CLASSICS
Illustrated®
Deluxe

THE SEA-WOLF

PAPERCUTZ™

CLASSICS ILLUSTRATED DELUXE
GRAPHIC NOVELS FROM PAPERCUTZ

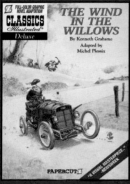

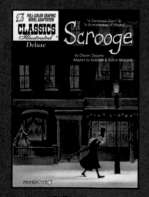

CLASSICS
Illustrated®
Deluxe

#11

THE SEA-WOLF

Jack London

Adapted by RIFF REB'S

PAPERCUTZ™
New York

"The Sea-Wolf"
By Jack London
Riff Reb's – Writer and Artist
Joe Johnson – Translation
Big Bird Zatryb – Lettering and Production
John Haufe and William B. Jones Jr. – Classics Illustrated Historians
Bryce Gold – Editorial Intern
Beth Scorzato – Production Coordinator
Michael Petranek – Editor
Jim Salicrup
Editor-in-Chief

ISBN: 978-1-59707-380-6 paperback edition
ISBN: 978-1-59707-401-8 hardcover edition

Papercutz books may be purchased for business or promotional use.
For information on bulk purchases please contact Macmillan Corporate
and Premium Sales Department at (800) 221-7945 x5442.

Printed in China
March 2014 by New Era Printing LTD.
Unit C, 8/F, Worldwide Centre
123 Tung Chau St., Kowloon, Hong Kong

Distributed by Macmillan
First Papercutz Printing

– Table of Contents –

I		9
II		25
III		41
IV		45
V		47
VI		51
VII		57
VIII		65
IX		73

X		79
XI		83
XII		93
XIII		101
XIV		117
XV		121
XVI		125
XVII		133

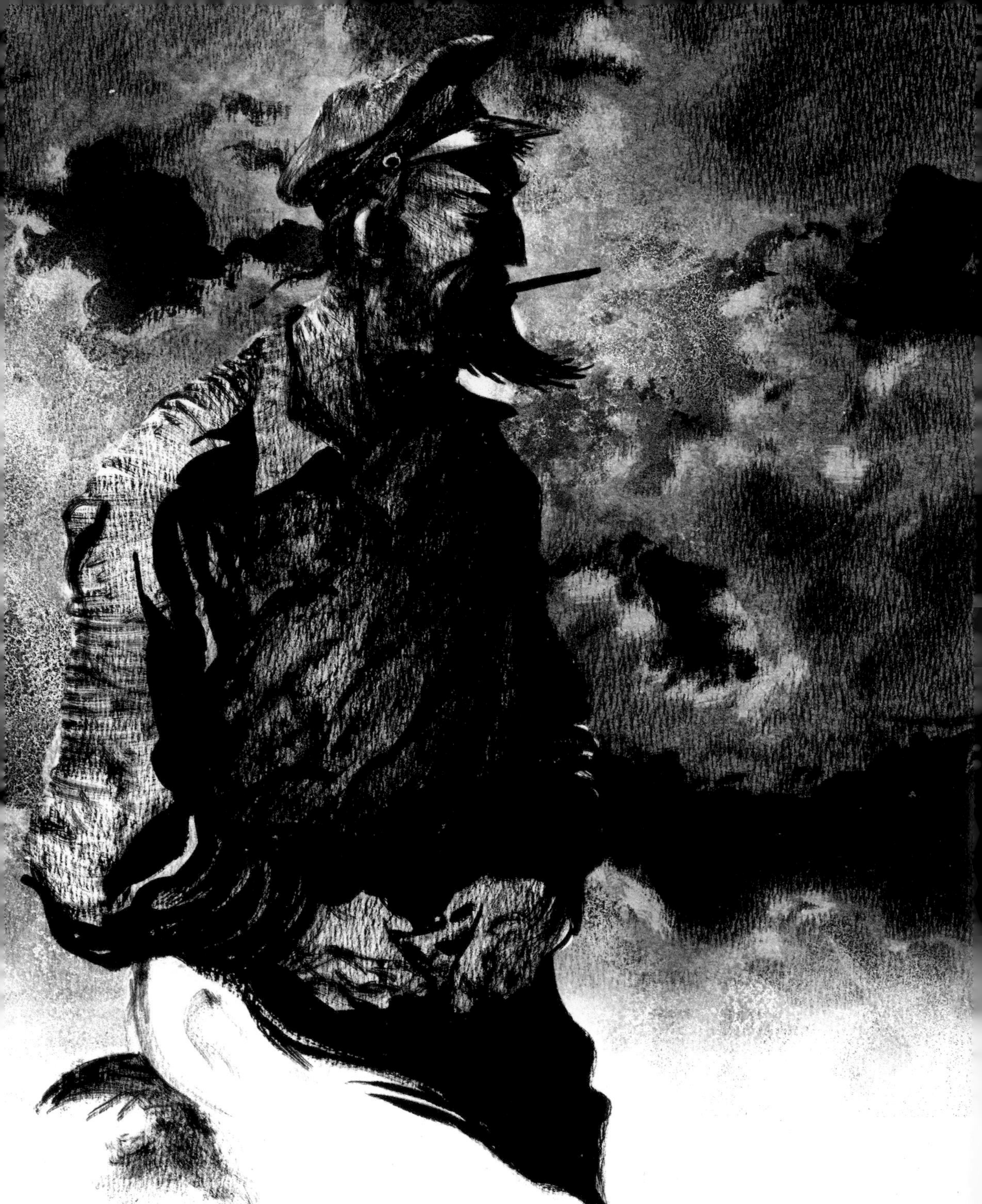

Preface

Jack London devoured life with the appetite of a raging fire:
An oyster poacher, seal-hunter, gold prospector, a revolutionary militant, vagrant,
war reporter, cattleman and farmer, a seaman on frigid seas and a yachtsman in warm
waters, a self-taught writer of more than fifty novels and short stories *(Martin Eden,
The Call of the Wild, The Star Rover, The Sea-Wolf...).*

Suddenly sated, he himself pisses on that fire like someone putting out a light,
at only forty years of age.

And this incredible assessment is hardly sufficient, for an author isn't
only the sum of his works and acts, but also that of his obsessions,
his wanderings, his dreams, as well as the ashes of his illusions.
Cooled ashes which warm us still, like those stars dead for millennia,
which shine yet to our eyes.

Riff Reb's

This work is dedicated to the memory
of Francis Lacassin, the preeminent, fascinating
preface writer of my greatest armchair voyages.

Riff Reb's

I

CROSSING SAN FRANCISCO BAY WAS ONLY A FORMALITY FOR ME. I LIKED TO MEET MY FRIEND CHARLEY FURUSETH TO EXPOUND UPON NIETZSCHE OR SCHOPENHAUER IN A SUMMER COTTAGE UNDER THE SHADOW OF MOUNT TAMALPAIS...

HAD IT NOT BEEN MY CUSTOM TO RUN UP AND SEE HIM EVERY SATURDAY AFTERNOON AND TO STOP OVER TILL MONDAY MORNING, THIS PARTICULAR JANUARY MONDAY MORNING WOULD NOT HAVE FOUND ME AFLOAT ON SAN FRANCISCO BAY.

HOW COULD I HAVE FORESEEN, AT THAT INSTANT, THAT A SIMPLE, ROUTINE VISIT WAS GOING TO RESHAPE THE VERY ESSENCE OF MY BEING?

NOT BUT THAT I WAS AFLOAT IN A SAFE CRAFT, FOR THE MARTINEZ WAS A NEW FERRY-STEAMER, MAKING HER FOURTH OR FIFTH TRIP ON THE RUN BETWEEN SAUSALITO AND SAN FRANCISCO.

THE DANGER LAY IN THE HEAVY FOG WHICH BLANKETED THE BAY, AND OF WHICH, AS A LANDSMAN, I HAD LITTLE APPREHENSION...

I REMEMBER THINKING HOW COMFORTABLE IT WAS, THIS DIVISION OF LABOR. ENTIRELY IGNORANT OF NAVIGATION, LIKE THE MAJORITY OF THE PASSENGERS, I ENTRUSTED MY LIFE TO THE PECULIAR KNOWLEDGE OF THE PILOT AND CAPTAIN.

?

THE DIVISION OF LABOR WAS IN FULL OPERATION. A STOUT GENTLEMAN, HAVING ABANDONED THE RESPONSIBILITY OF THE TRANSPORTATION OF HIS BODY TO THE SPECIALISTS OF THE SEA, COULD FULLY DEVOTE HIS MIND TO READING THE ARTICLE I'D WRITTEN, ME, A SPECIALIST ON EDGAR ALLAN POE.

TOC TOC TOC

TOC TOC

TOC TOC

TOC

-:MMMRRR--:-

IT'S NASTY WEATHER LIKE THIS HERE THAT TURNS HEADS GRAY BEFORE THEIR TIME....

I 4

I HAD NOT THOUGHT THERE WAS ANY PARTICULAR STRAIN. IT SEEMS AS SIMPLE AS A, B, C...

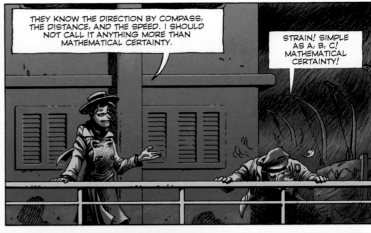

THEY KNOW THE DIRECTION BY COMPASS, THE DISTANCE, AND THE SPEED. I SHOULD NOT CALL IT ANYTHING MORE THAN MATHEMATICAL CERTAINTY.

STRAIN! SIMPLE AS A, B, C! MATHEMATICAL CERTAINTY!

DING DING DING DING

LISTEN TO THAT, WILL YOU? A BELL-BUOY, AND WE'RE A-TOP OF IT! IT SHOULD BE TO THE STARBOARD!

SEE 'EM ALTERIN' THE COURSE! HA! HA! HA! MATHEMATICAL CERTAINTY, THAT'S A GOOD ONE!

MAR... EZ

DING DING

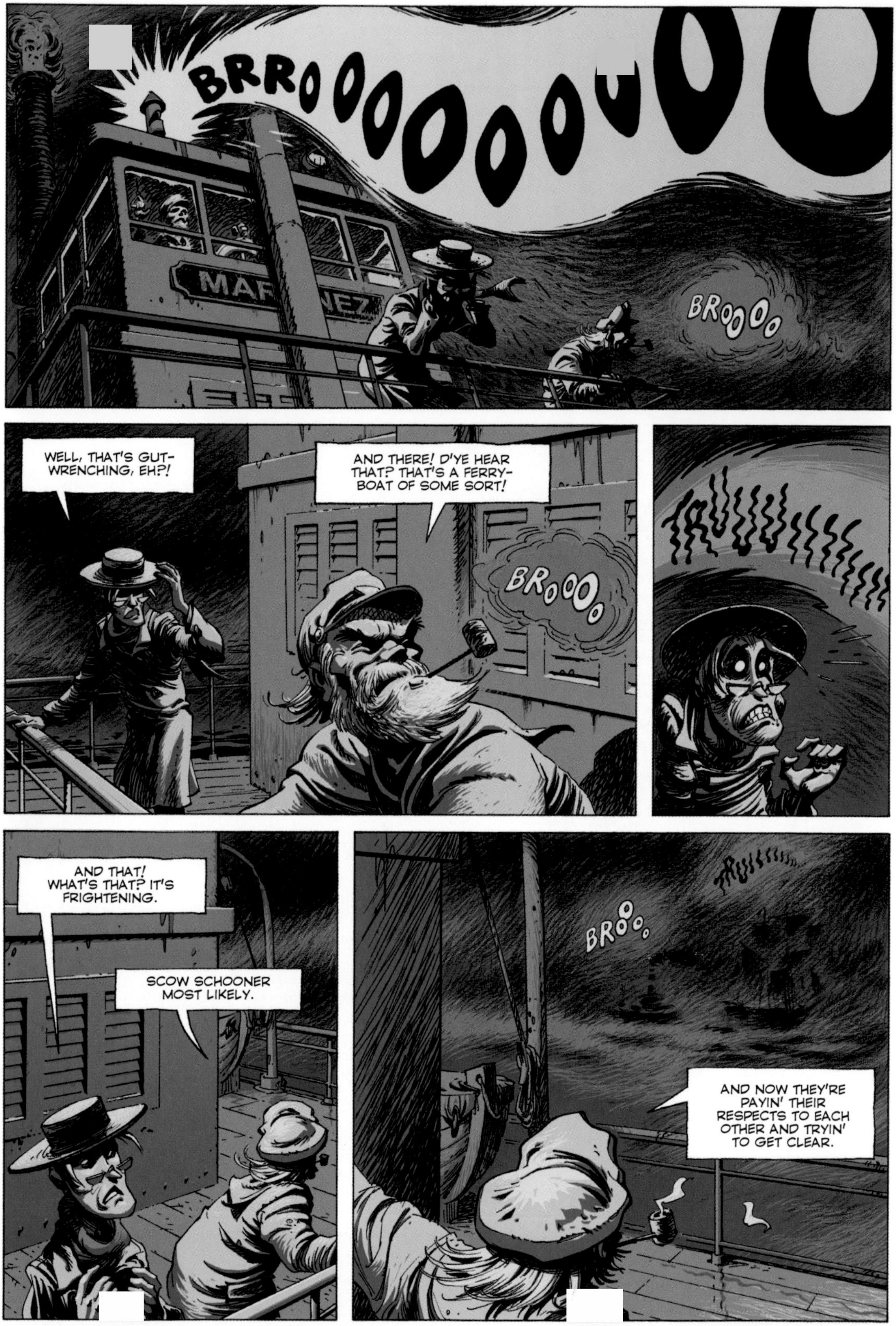
BRROOOOOOOOOO
MARTINEZ
BROOOO
WELL, THAT'S GUT-WRENCHING, EH?!
AND THERE! D'YE HEAR THAT? THAT'S A FERRY-BOAT OF SOME SORT!
BROOOO
TRUUUIIII
AND THAT! WHAT'S THAT? IT'S FRIGHTENING.
SCOW SCHOONER MOST LIKELY.
BROOO
AND NOW THEY'RE PAYIN' THEIR RESPECTS TO EACH OTHER AND TRYIN' TO GET CLEAR.

I 6

YOU REMIND ME OF MY GRANDFATHER. HE RECOGNIZED BIRDS BY THEIR SONG.

-:MMRRR:-, THERE ARE ONLY BIRDS OF ILL OMEN HERE...

AND YOU WOULDN'T GET ULYSSES TO BELIEVE THAT SIRENS ARE JUST BIRDS!

I FELT QUITE AMUSED AT HIS UNWARRANTED CHOLER, AND WHILE HE STUMPED INDIGNANTLY UP AND DOWN I FELL TO DWELLING UPON THE ROMANCE OF THE FOG...

AND ROMANTIC IT CERTAINLY WAS-- THE FOG, LIKE THE GRAY SHADOW OF INFINITE MYSTERY, BROODING OVER THE WHIRLING SPECK OF EARTH...

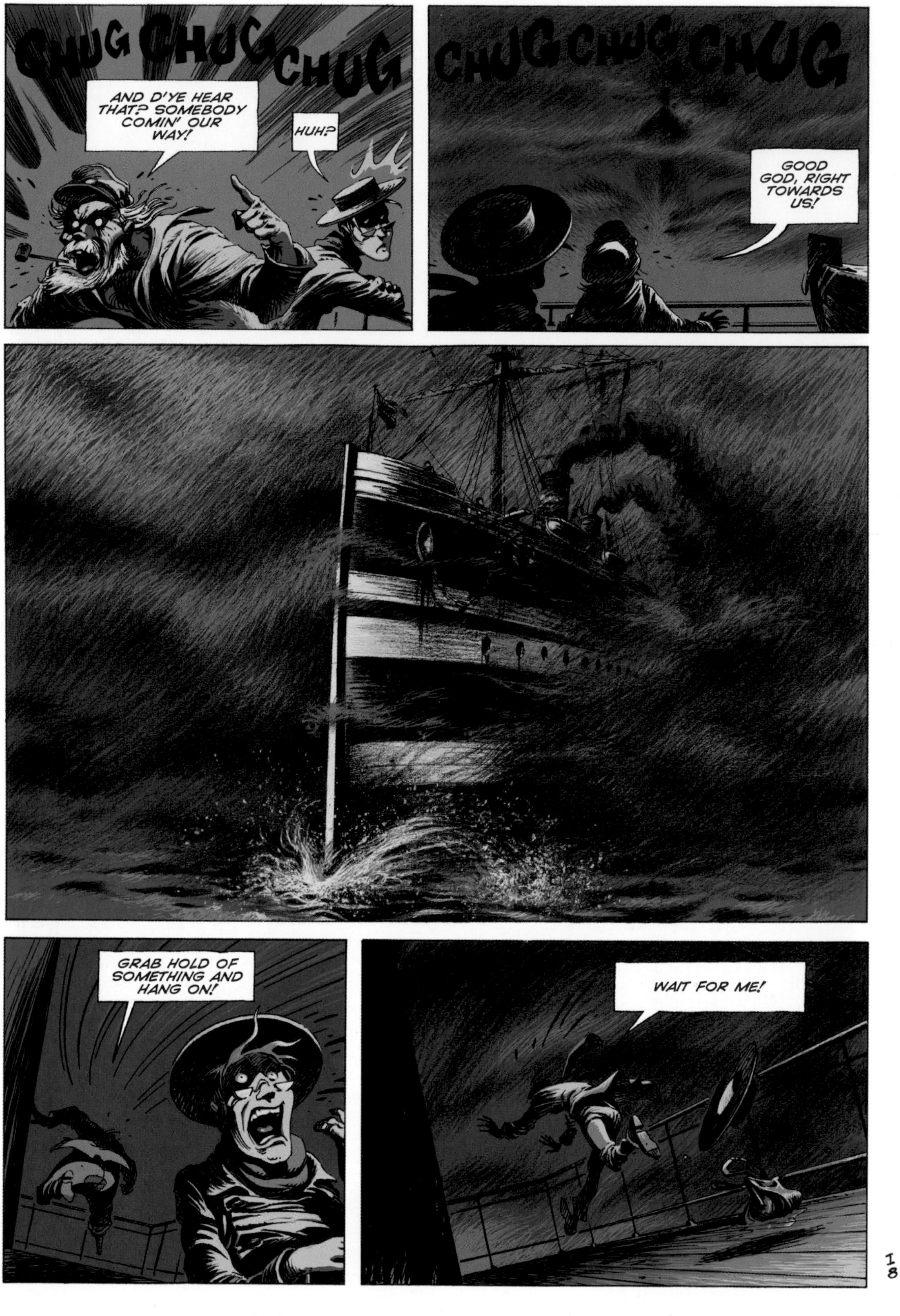
CHUG CHUG CHUG
AND D'YE HEAR THAT? SOMEBODY COMIN' OUR WAY!
HUH?
CHUG CHUG CHUG
GOOD GOD, RIGHT TOWARDS US!
GRAB HOLD OF SOMETHING AND HANG ON!
WAIT FOR ME!
18

HELP ME! PASS OUT THE LIFE PRESERVERS!

WHAT WAS HAPPENING TO ME? ASSAULTED BY REALITY, I WAS STUNNED ON MY FEET. I WASN'T TRAVELING THROUGH LITERATURE ANY LONGER!

WELL! GET A MOVE ON!

I LIVED THROUGH THE REST IN A DAZE...

IS THE SITUATION SO WORRISOME THAT EVERYONE MUST SCREAM?

I
10

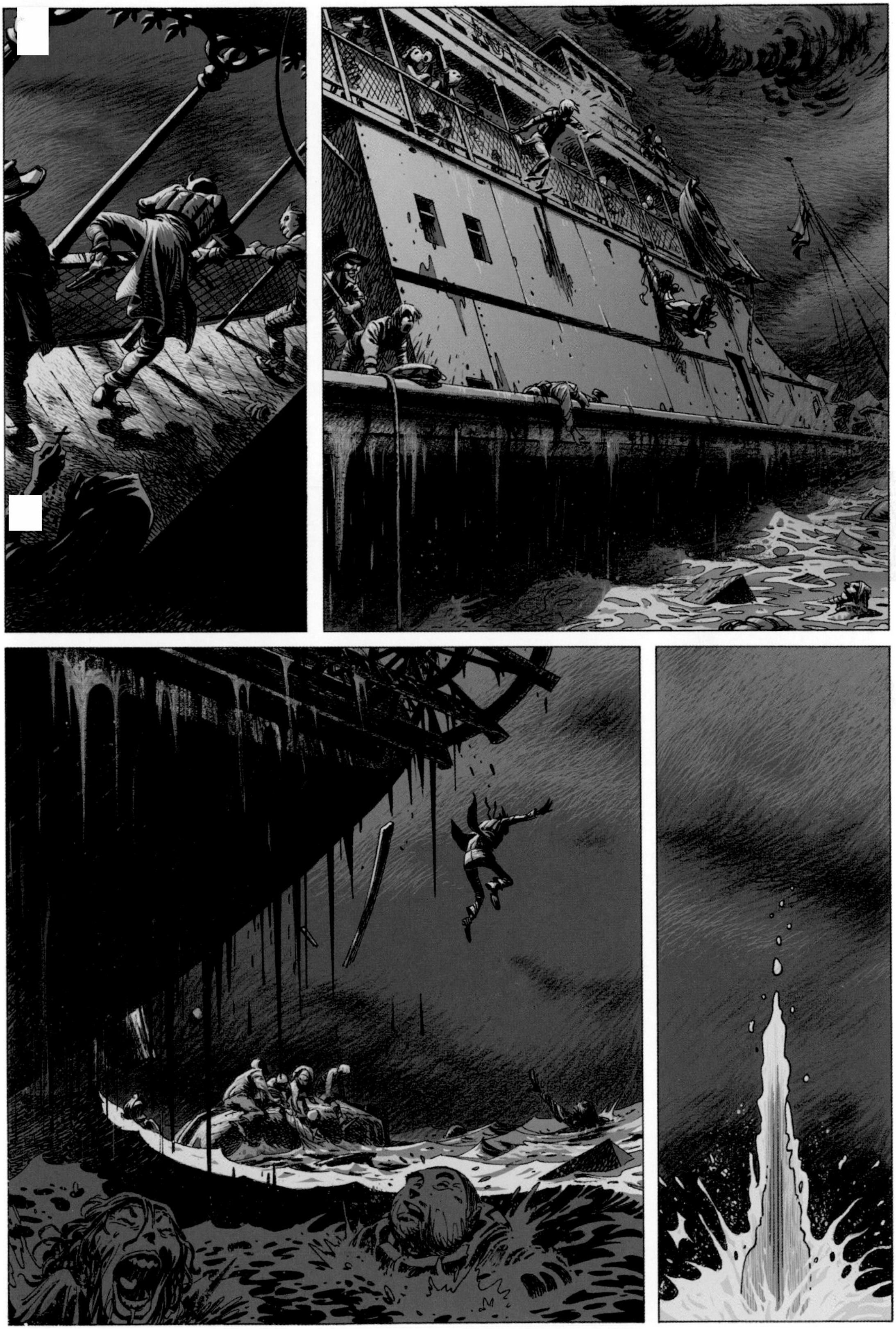

I 11

THE WATER WAS COLD-- SO COLD IT WAS PAINFUL. THE PANG WAS AS QUICK AND SHARP AS THAT OF FIRE. IT BIT TO THE MARROW.

WITHOUT ME UNDERSTANDING HOW OR WHY, THE CURRENT RAPIDLY CARRIED ME FAR FROM THE TEEMING CHORUS OF SCREAMS...

AND I HEARD, ALSO, THE SOUND OF OARS. EVIDENTLY THE STRANGE STEAMBOAT HAD LOWERED ITS BOATS...

I WAS ALONE, VOICELESS. THE MARTINEZ HAD GONE DOWN AND I LOST CONSCIOUSNESS...

I
12

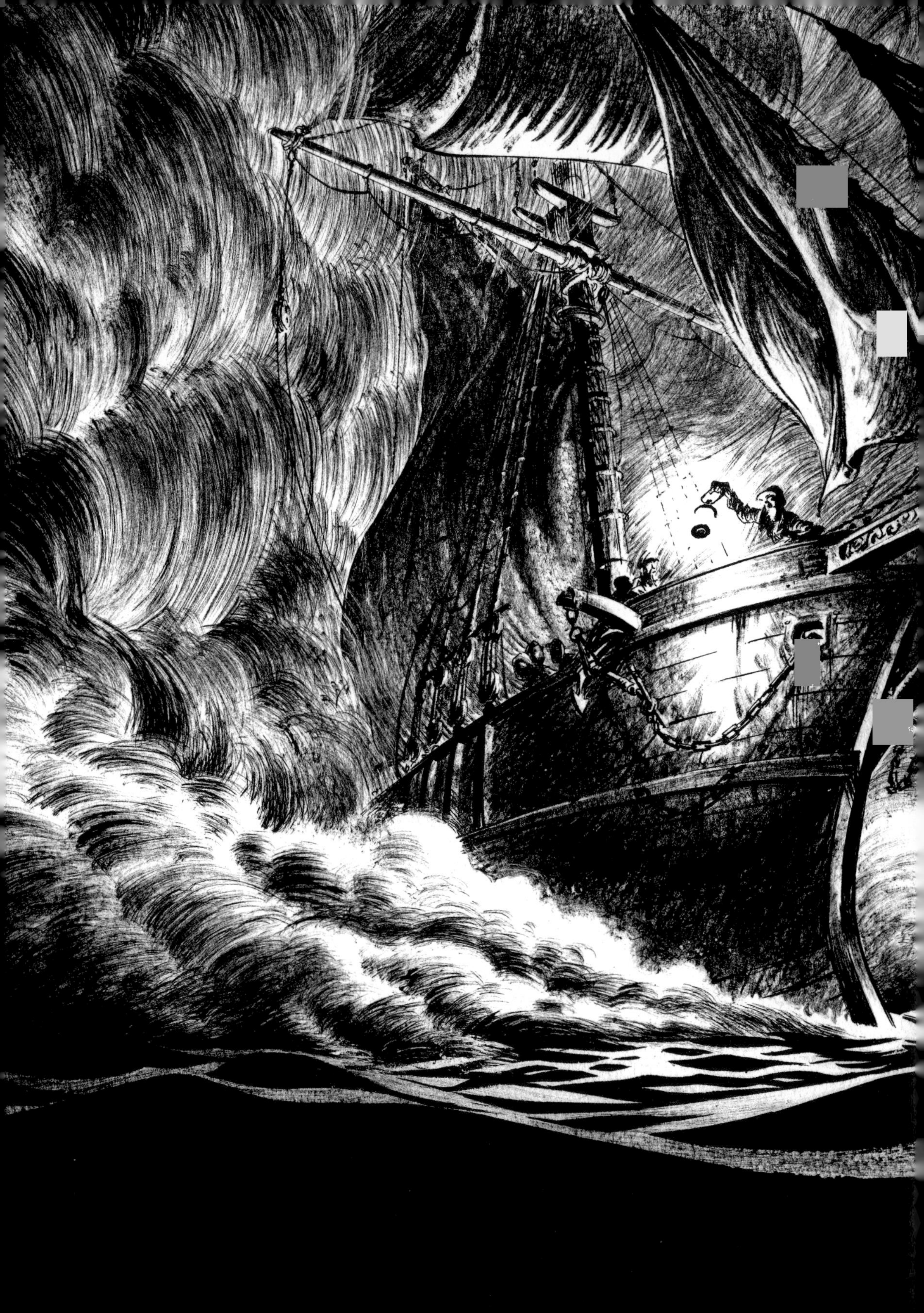

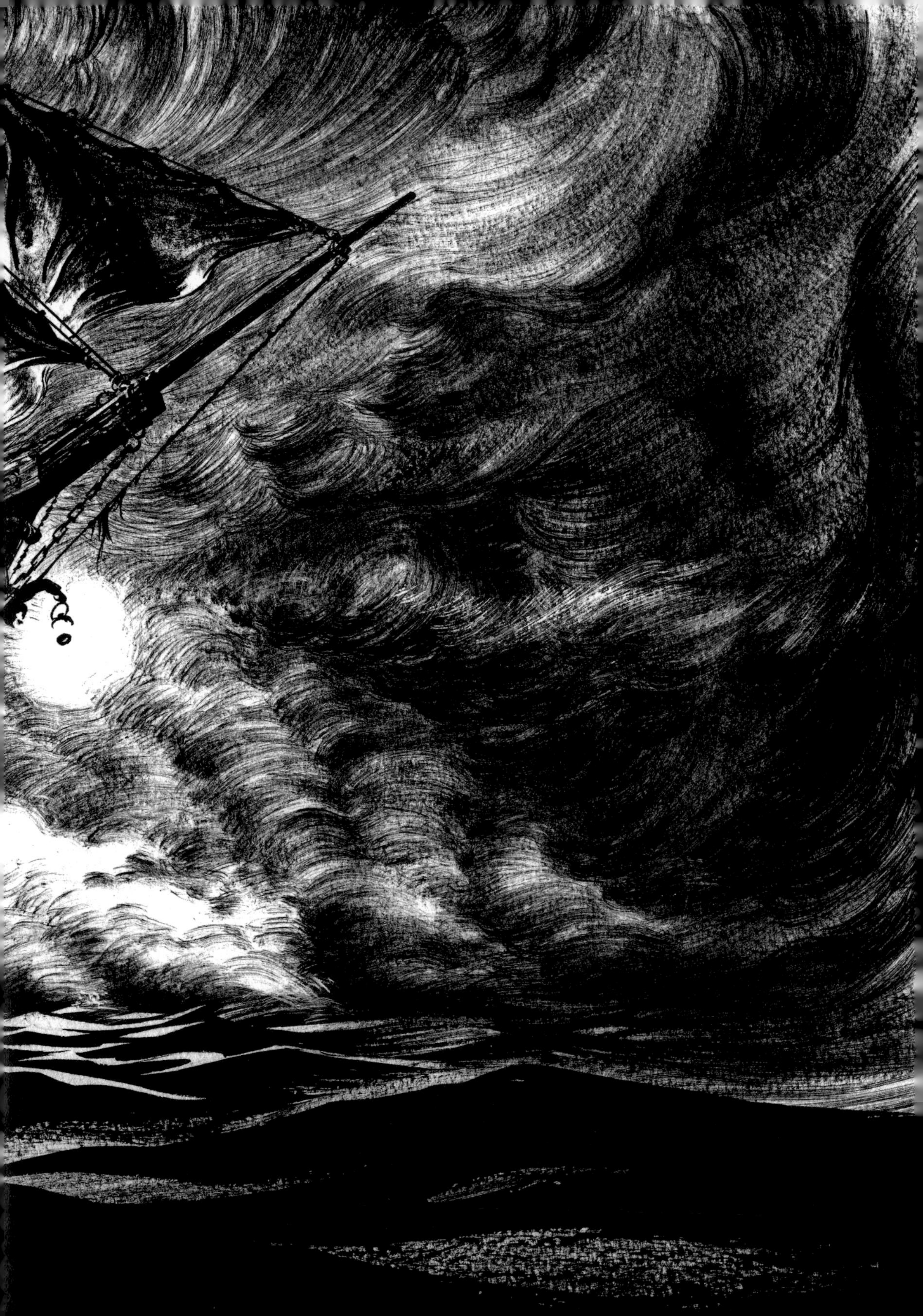

II

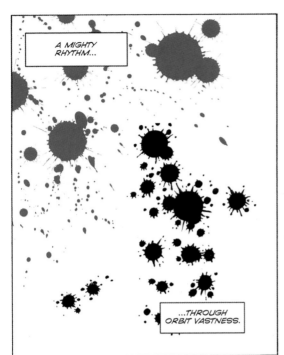

A MIGHTY RHYTHM...

...THROUGH ORBIT VASTNESS.

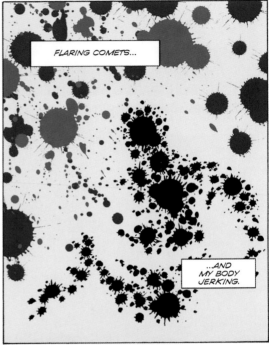

FLARING COMETS...

...AND MY BODY JERKING.

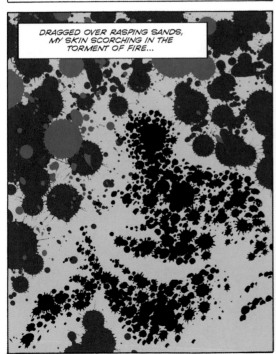

DRAGGED OVER RASPING SANDS, MY SKIN SCORCHING IN THE TORMENT OF FIRE...

AAAAAAAAAAAGH!

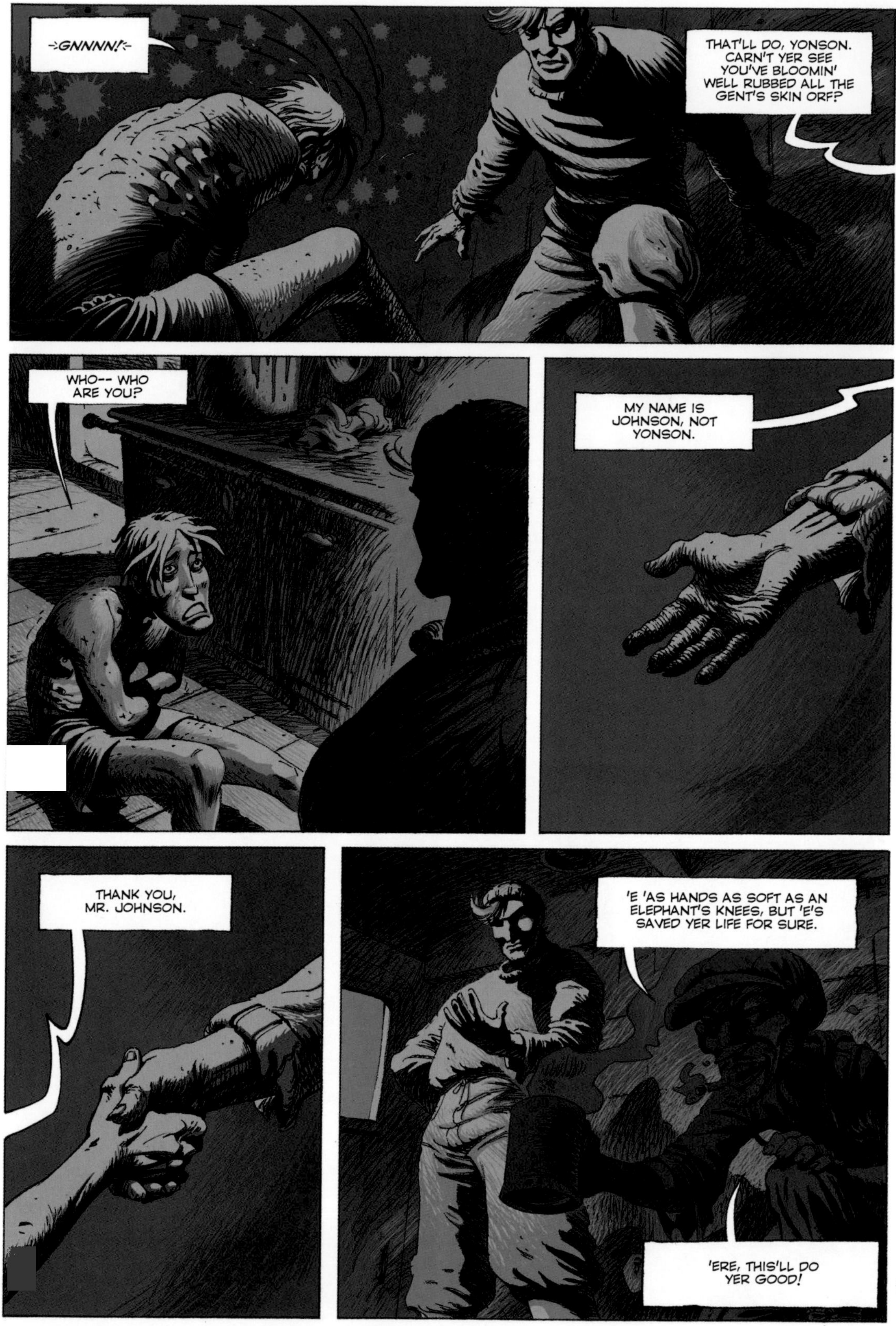

GNNNN!
THAT'LL DO, YONSON. CARN'T YER SEE YOU'VE BLOOMIN' WELL RUBBED ALL THE GENT'S SKIN ORF?
WHO-- WHO ARE YOU?
MY NAME IS JOHNSON, NOT YONSON.
THANK YOU, MR. JOHNSON.
'E 'AS HANDS AS SOFT AS AN ELEPHANT'S KNEES, BUT 'E'S SAVED YER LIFE FOR SURE.
'ERE, THIS'LL DO YER GOOD!

II 2

AND WHERE AM I?

SNIF

THE SCHOONER *GHOST*, BOUND SEAL-HUNTING TO JAPAN.

JAPAN?!

HAVE YOU ANY DRY CLOTHES I MAY PUT ON?

YES, SIR. IF YOU'VE NO OBJECTIONS, SIR, TO WEARIN' MY THINGS.

AND WHO IS THE CAPTAIN? I MUST SEE HIM AS SOON AS I AM DRESSED.

YOU DON'T KNOW HIS NAME? IS THERE A PROBLEM?

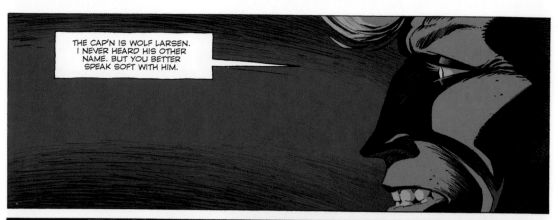

THE CAP'N IS WOLF LARSEN. I NEVER HEARD HIS OTHER NAME. BUT YOU BETTER SPEAK SOFT WITH HIM.

WHILE THE SAILOR JOHNSON WON ME OVER IMMEDIATELY, THE COOK STRAIGHTAWAY INSPIRED A PROFOUND DISLIKE ACCENTUATED BY HIS OBSEQUIOUS MANNERS...

HOW DO YOU EXPLAIN WHAT HAPPENED TO THESE TROUSERS?

THEY WAS PUT AW'Y WET, SIR. BUT YOU'LL 'AVE TO MAKE THEM DO TILL I DRY YOURS OUT BY THE FIRE.

AND WHOM HAVE I TO THANK FOR THIS KINDNESS?

MUGRIDGE, SIR. THOMAS MUGRIDGE.

ALL RIGHT, THOMAS, I SHALL NOT FORGET YOU WHEN MY CLOTHES ARE DRY.

STAGGERING STILL, I STEPPED ONTO THE DECK IN MY RIDICULOUS ACCOUTREMENT...

II
4

28

THE SCHOONER WAS BOWING AND PLUNGING INTO THE LONG PACIFIC ROLL...

LOOKING AFT, I COULD MAKE OUT THE NARROW SLICE OF THE CALIFORNIAN COAST AND SEE THE FOG BANK'S THAT HAD BROUGHT ABOUT THE DISASTER TO THE MARTINEZ...

TO FORE, THE OPEN SEA, A GROUP OF NAKED ROCK'S AND THE PYRAMIDAL LOOM OF SOME VESSEL'S SAILS...

I READIED MYSELF TO FACE THE CAPTAIN "WOLF LARSEN," SURPRISED THAT THE SURVIVOR OF A CATASTROPHE SUCH AS I HAD MERITED SO LITTLE ATTENTION...

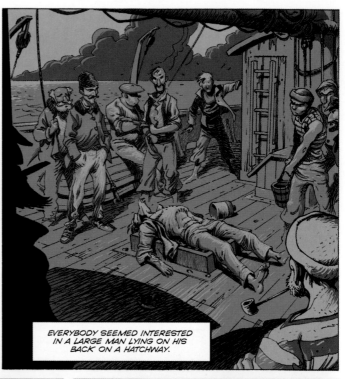

EVERYBODY SEEMED INTERESTED IN A LARGE MAN LYING ON HIS BACK ON A HATCHWAY.

HIS EYES CLOSED, HIS MOUTH WIDE OPEN, HE LABORED NOISILY FOR BREATH.

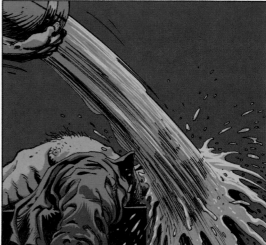

II 6

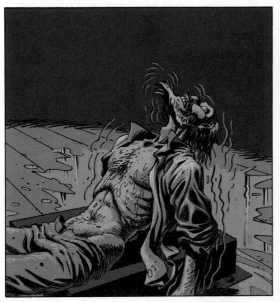

AT THE MOMENT WHEN THE WRETCH BREATHED HIS LAST, A MASSIVE SILHOUETTE I'D NOT HERETOFORE REMARKED DETACHED ITSELF FROM THE SHADOW OF THE MASTS...

BEYOND ALL DOUBT, THIS COLOSSUS REMINISCENT OF SOME TREE-DWELLING PROTOTYPE WAS WOLF LARSEN...

HOW'S IT POSSIBLE A SCUM-SUCKING SON OF A WITCH, A SOT FROM BIRTH COULD DIE, FROM DRINKING TOO MUCH?!

FLAPPING AROUND LIKE COD ON DORY PLANKS-- WHAT A RIDICULOUS END FOR A SEAMAN!

WITH A TURN FOR LITERARY EXPRESSION MYSELF, AND A PENCHANT FOR FORCIBLE FIGURES AND PHRASES, I APPRECIATED THE PECULIAR VIVIDNESS AND STRENGTH AND ABSOLUTE BLASPHEMY OF HIS METAPHORS. I WILL SPARE YOU THE ESSENTIALS OF THIS EXPLOSION OF INDECENCY-- AGAINST A DEAD MAN...

GO ON AND SMILE, RABBIT DUNG-- DOING THIS TO ME, AT THE BEGINNING OF THE VOYAGE!

MUGRIDGE, YOU'VE STRETCHED YOUR NECK ENOUGH. IT'S UNHEALTHY, YOU KNOW! I'VE ALREADY LOST MY MATE! GO BELOW AND FILL A SACK WITH COAL!

JOHANSEN! GET YOUR PALM AND NEEDLE AND SEW THE BEGGAR UP! YOU'LL FIND SOME OLD CANVAS IN THE SAIL-LOCKER!

ANY OF YOU FELLOWS GOT A BIBLE OR A PRAYER-BOOK? THIS IDIOT, TO TOP OFF ALL HIS FAULTS, THOUGHT FIT TO BELIEVE IN GOD!

II
8

GOD IS EVERYWHERE, WHY BOTHER WITH A BOOK?!

HA! HA! HA! HA! HA! HA!

THEN WE'LL DROP HIM OVER WITHOUT ANY PALAVERING, UNLESS OUR CLERICAL-LOOKING CASTAWAY HAS THE BURIAL SERVICE AT SEA BY HEART?

YOU'RE A PREACHER, AREN'T YOU?

NO-- NOT AT ALL, I--

WHAT DO YOU DO FOR A LIVING?

I--I AM A GENTLEMAN. I HAVE AN INCOME.

WHO EARNED IT? EH? I THOUGHT SO. YOUR FATHER. YOU STAND ON DEAD MEN'S LEGS.

II
9

33

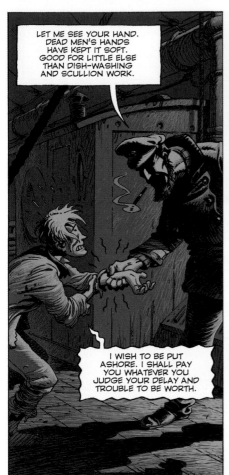

LET ME SEE YOUR HAND. DEAD MEN'S HANDS HAVE KEPT IT SOFT. GOOD FOR LITTLE ELSE THAN DISH-WASHING AND SCULLION WORK.

I WISH TO BE PUT ASHORE. I SHALL PAY YOU WHATEVER YOU JUDGE YOUR DELAY AND TROUBLE TO BE WORTH.

I HAVE A COUNTER PROPOSITION TO MAKE. MY MATE'S GONE, AND THERE'LL BE A LOT OF PROMOTION, THE CABIN-BOY, TOO. YOU'LL TAKE HIS PLACE, TWENTY DOLLARS PER MONTH AND FOUND.

IT WILL BE THE MAKING OF YOU. YOU MIGHT LEARN IN TIME TO STAND ON YOUR OWN LEGS.

LIKE A MATCHSTICK IN A VISE! MY ARM WOULD MAKE ME SUFFER FOR SEVERAL WEEKS. AND YET, WOLF LARSEN HAD EXERTED BUT A MODERATE PRESSURE.

CABIN-BOY! WHERE'S THE CABIN-BOY?

THE VESSEL I'D SEEN OFF TO THE SOUTHWEST WAS DRAWING CLOSER. IT WAS MY LAST CHANCE TO RETURN TO SAN FRANCISCO.

II
10

HERE I AM.

WHAT'S YOUR NAME, BOY?

GEORGE LEACH, SIR.

NOT AN IRISH NAME. O'TOOLE OR MCCARTHY WOULD SUIT YOUR MUG A DAMN SIGHT BETTER. UNLESS, VERY LIKELY, THERE'S AN IRISHMAN IN YOUR MOTHER'S WOODPILE. HOW OLD ARE YOU?

SIXTEEN!

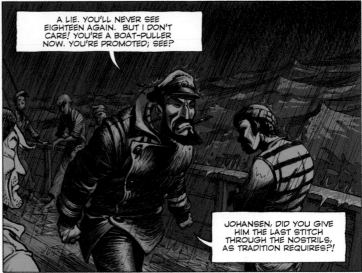

A LIE. YOU'LL NEVER SEE EIGHTEEN AGAIN. BUT I DON'T CARE! YOU'RE A BOAT-PULLER NOW. YOU'RE PROMOTED; SEE?

JOHANSEN, DID YOU GIVE HIM THE LAST STITCH THROUGH THE NOSTRILS, AS TRADITION REQUIRES?!

UH-- NOTHING AT ALL!

DO YOU KNOW ANYTHING ABOUT NAVIGATION?

WELL, NEVER MIND; YOU'RE MATE JUST THE SAME.

AY, AY, SIR!

WHAT ARE YOU WAITING FOR?

I DIDN'T SIGN FOR BOAT-PULLER, SIR. I SIGNED FOR CABIN-BOY.

CAP--UMM, CAPTAIN! WHAT VESSEL IS THAT?

II
12

THE PILOT-BOAT *LADY MINE*. RUNNING INTO SAN FRANCISCO IN FIVE OR SIX HOURS.

WILL YOU PLEASE SIGNAL IT, THEN, SO THAT I MAY BE PUT ASHORE?

SORRY. BUT I'VE LOST THE SIGNAL BOOK OVERBOARD WHEN I LEANED OVER TO SAVE YOUR LIFE.

LADY MINE AHOY! A THOUSAND DOLLARS IF YOU TAKE ME ASHORE!

?

WHAT IS THE MATTER?

TOO MUCH 'FRISCO TANGLEFOOT FOR THE HEALTH OF MY CABIN-BOY! HE FANCIES SEA-SERPENTS AND MONKEYS JUST NOW!

UNDERSTOOD! HA HA HA! GIVE HIM HELL FOR ME!

II
13

EVERYONE ON DECK, NOW THAT WE'VE EVERYTHING CLEANED UP!

WHAT IS YOUR NAME?

HUMPHREY VAN WEYDEN.

THAT'LL DO, HUMP. GO TO THE COOK AND LEARN YOUR DUTIES ONCE WE'VE FINISHED WITH THIS MOVING FUNERAL SERVICE.

CAPS OFF, YOU HERD OF SWINE, WE'RE TOSSING ONE OF OUR OWN FOR CHUM, AFTER ALL!

II
14

IS THE SACK OF COAL TIED TO HIS FEET WELL?

I ONLY REMEMBER ONE PART OF THE SERVICE AND THAT IS "AND THE BODY SHALL BE CAST INTO THE SEA."

SO, CAST IT IN! WHAT THE HELL'S THE MATTER WITH YOU?

JOHANSEN! GET IN THE TOPSAILS AND JIBS AND MAKE A GOOD JOB OF IT. WE'RE IN FOR A SOU'EASTER. BETTER REEF THE JIB AND MAINSAIL, TOO.

II
15

I STAYED THERE, AMID THE COMMOTION, AS TERRIFIED AS A HATCHLING IN HELL. IF EDGAR ALLAN POE HAD INVENTED HORROR STORIES, WHAT WAS I EXPERIENCING?

CLINGING TO THE SHROUDS, MY EYES SOUGHT THE COAST OF MY COUNTRY, BUT IN VAIN. CIVILIZATION HAD DISAPPEARED, ERASED BY THE RAINSQUALLS.

THE GHOST, EVER LEAPING UP AND OUT, WAS HEADING AWAY INTO THE SOUTHWEST, INTO THE GREAT AND LONELY PACIFIC EXPANSE.

II
16

III

I WAS SENT TO SLEEP IN THE STEERAGE AMONG THE HUNTERS. TIRED AS I WAS, I WAS PREVENTED FROM SLEEPING BY MY INFLAMED SKIN AND THE PAIN IN MY KNEE...

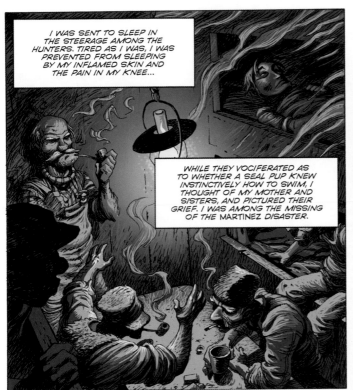

WHILE THEY VOCIFERATED AS TO WHETHER A SEAL PUP KNEW INSTINCTIVELY HOW TO SWIM, I THOUGHT OF MY MOTHER AND SISTERS, AND PICTURED THEIR GRIEF. I WAS AMONG THE MISSING OF THE MARTINEZ DISASTER.

ENVELOPED IN AN OFFENSIVE-SMELLING CLOUD OF CHEAP TOBACCO, I IMAGINED MYSELF SIMULTANEOUSLY DEAD AND A CABIN-BOY TRYING TO BRAG ABOUT MY PROMOTION TO MY APPALLED FRIEND CHARLEY FURUSETH.

I SWEAR TO YOU, CHARLEY. EVERYTHING'S FINE! IT'S A REWARDING EXPERIENCE--

AND IT WAS A LONG, LONG NIGHT, WEARY AND DREARY AND LONG.

UP WITH YE, NO MORE LIVING IN A CASTLE!

SHUT UP, MUGRIDGE!

CH'TOC

OWWW!

MY APOLOGIES, SORRY, SORRY! IT WON'T HAPPEN AGAIN!

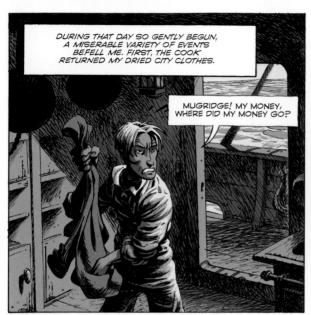

DURING THAT DAY SO GENTLY BEGUN, A MISERABLE VARIETY OF EVENTS BEFELL ME. FIRST, THE COOK RETURNED MY DRIED CITY CLOTHES.

MUGRIDGE! MY MONEY, WHERE DID MY MONEY GO?

THAS *MISTER* MUGRIDGE! D'YE WANT YER NOSE PUNCHED? IF YOU THINK I'M A THIEF, JUST KEEP IT TO YERSELF.

'ER YOU COME, A PORE MIS'RABLE SPECIMEN OF 'UMAN SCUM, AN' I TYKES YER INTO MY GALLEY AN' TREATS YER 'ANSOM, AN' THIS IS WOT I GET FOR IT.

'UMP!

THEREAFTER, FORE AND AFT, I WAS KNOWN BY NO OTHER NAME. UNTIL THE TERM BECAME PART OF MY THOUGHT-PROCESS AND I IDENTIFIED IT WITH MYSELF.

AFTER BREAKFAST, I HAD ANOTHER UNENVIABLE EXPERIENCE. I FLUNG THE ASHES FROM THE CABIN STOVE OVER THE SIDE TO WINDWARD.

THE WIND DROVE THEM BACK OVER WOLF LARSEN. I HAD NOT REALIZED THERE COULD BE SO MUCH PAIN IN A KICK.

III
2

LATER IN THE MORNING I RECEIVED A SURPRISE OF A TOTALLY DIFFERENT SORT, WHILE CLEANING WOLF LARSEN'S STATEROOM.

BOOKS! AND WHAT BOOKS! SHAKESPEARE, TENNYSON, POE, DE QUINCEY, DARWIN, PROCTOR, ASTRONOMY, PHYSICS, AND MOST AMUSING, A COPY OF "THE DEAN'S ENGLISH!"

I COULD NOT RECONCILE THESE BOOKS WITH THE MAN FROM WHAT I'D SEEN OF HIM.

WERE MY BOOKS IN SUCH NEED OF DUSTING?

UH-- I-I'VE BEEN ROBBED! UH-- CAPTAIN. MUGRIDGE TOOK THE MONEY I HAD WHEN YOU SAVED MY LIFE!

COOKY'S PICKINGS. AND DON'T YOU THINK YOUR MISERABLE LIFE IS WORTH THE PRICE?

BESIDES, YOU HAVE SINNED.

HOW'S THAT?

YOU TEMPTED COOKY, AND HE FELL. YOU HAVE PLACED HIS IMMORTAL SOUL IN JEOPARDY. BY THE WAY, DO YOU BELIEVE IN THE IMMORTAL SOUL?

III
3

I READ IMMORTALITY IN YOUR EYES.

HA! HA! HA! RUBBISH! ALL THAT YOU CAN SEE IS THAT I'M ALIVE!

THE IMMORTALITY OF THE SOUL IS A SONG AND DANCE FOR COWARDS AND THE NAÏVE!

I'LL TELL YOU THE CORE OF MY THOUGHT. MAN IS A MEDIOCRE ANIMAL, AND WITHOUT THE APPEARANCE OF CONSCIOUSNESS, HE'D HAVE LONG SINCE DISAPPEARED FROM THIS PLANET. BUT THE PRICE TO PAY IS CONSCIOUSNESS OF HIS OWN DEATH, AND THAT'S A HEAVY ONE!

SO, HE INVENTED THE IDEA OF IMMORTALITY TO ACCEPT THIS INEVITABLE ENDING AND THE IDEA OF THE SOUL TO ESTABLISH HIS SO-CALLED SUPERIORITY OVER THE ANIMAL KINGDOM.

I BELIEVE NEITHER IN GOD NOR IN MAN!

THAT'S NIHILISM!

I KNOW!

BY THE WAY, HOW MUCH WAS IT THAT COOKY GOT AWAY WITH?

ONE HUNDRED AND EIGHTY-FIVE DOLLARS, SIR.

CURSE IT, YOU HALFWITTED BOSUN, LET GO OF THAT BLACKGUARD JOHANSEN!

III
4

44

IV

I, HUMPHREY VAN WEYDEN, A DILETTANTE OF THE PEN, A SPECIALIST IN ART AND LITERATURE, WAS EMPLOYED AT THE LEVEL IN WHICH SUCH SKILLS COULD PROVIDE FOR THIS SHIP OF BRUTES: I WAS PEELING POTATOES AND SCRAPING GREASE FROM DISHES.

THUS, TO THE ENDLESS SARCASMS OF THAT DISGRACE OF HUMANITY THAT WAS "MISTER" MUGRIDGE, THE DAYS RAN TOGETHER.

THE POOR, LITTLE 'UMP'S 'ANDS 'URT!

IV
1

ON TUESDAY, I MADE THE ACQUAINTANCE OF LOUIS THE "BABBLER," WHO DOES IN FACT TALK A LOT...

NOBODY'S ON THIS BOAT OF HIS OWN FREE WILL, HUMP. WOLF IS THE GREAT BIG BEAST OF THE APOCALYPSE, AND THE SECOND MATE WON'T BE THE ONLY ONE NOT TO RETURN HOME, I CAN TELL YOU!

WEDNESDAY, WOLF LARSEN CAME AND MADE AN IMPRESSIVE, RIDICULOUS DEMONSTRATION OF STRENGTH IN THE GALLEY BY CRUSHING A RAW POTATO IN HIS RIGHT HAND...

I'M POCKETING THE BETS; YOU SEND THE MONEY.

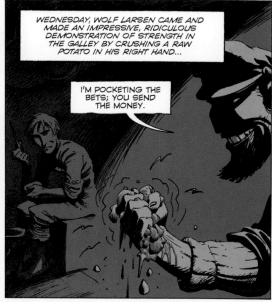

THURSDAY, TO THE GREAT AMUSEMENT OF THE CAPTAIN, YOUNG HARRISON SPENT FOUR HOURS CLUTCHING THE END OF THE SPAR DURING ROUGH WEATHER BEFORE COMING DOWN ALIVE, BUT TRAUMATIZED.

FRIDAY, A HEAVY CLOUD CAST A SHADOW OVER RELATIONS BETWEEN THE COURAGEOUS JOHNSON AND WOLF LARSEN.

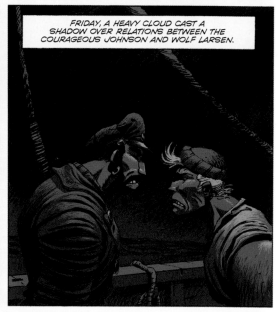

AND I, THE MAN FROM THE HIGHEST REALMS OF INTELLECTUALISM-- I WAS PEELING POTATOES.

IV
2

V

HERE'S HOW, IN A FEW WORDS, A MADMAN OR A GENIUS TRANSFORMS THE MAGIC OF AN IDEAL NIGHT INTO AN ABYSS OF DESPAIR.

AT LAST, AFTER THREE DAYS OF VARIABLE WINDS, WE HAVE THE NORTHEAST TRADES. THE SCHOONER SAILED HERSELF.

IN THE HUMIDITY OF THAT EVENING, THE SEA RENT BY THE BOW CAST A SPECTRAL RIPPLE OF FOAM THAT SOUNDED LIKE THE GURGLING OF A BROOK IN SOME QUIET DELL.

"O THE BLAZING TROPIC NIGHT, WHEN THE WAKE'S A WELT OF LIGHT THAT HOLDS THE HOT SKY TAME, AND THE STEADY FOREFOOT SNORES--

?

V
1

47

"--THROUGH THE PLANET-POWDERED FLOORS WHERE THE SCARED WHALE FLUKES IN FLAME. HER PLATES ARE SCARRED BY THE SUN, DEAR LASS, AND HER ROPES ARE TAUT WITH THE DEW--

"FOR WE'RE BOOMING DOWN ON THE OLD TRAIL, OUR OWN TRAIL, THE OUT TRAIL--

"'WE'RE SAGGING SOUTH ON THE LONG TRAIL-- THE TRAIL THAT IS ALWAYS NEW."

WELL, IT SEEMS THAT LIFE UNDER THE TRADE-WINDS DOESN'T INSPIRE LITERARY CRITICISM!

IT STRIKES ME AS REMARKABLE YOU SHOULD SHOW ENTHUSIASM. ACCORDING TO YOU, LIFE IS WITHOUT VALUE.

--ARF! ARF!-- OUR FLEDGLING IS GETTING HIS FEATHERS!

OF COURSE LIFE IS VALUELESS, EXCEPT TO ITSELF.

MY LIFE OF YESTERDAY IS NO LONGER WORTH ANYTHING, THAT OF TOMORROW IS WORTH NOTHING YET AND, JUST NOW, IN THE SWEETNESS OF THIS LOVELY NIGHT, IT IS BEYOND PRICE!

IT WOULD CERTAINLY BE EASIER AND MORE AMUSING TO KNOW THE PRICE YOU'RE READY TO PAY TO SEE ME DEAD THAN TO HEM AND HAW OVER THE VALUE OF A LIFE.

I BELIEVE IN THE SURVIVAL OF THE SOUL AND I WISH FOR NO ONE'S DEATH.

BAH! WHAT A PLATITUDE! I BELIEVE IN POETRY AND RECOMMEND READING RUDYARD KIPLING TO YOU!

AN ABYSS OF DESPAIR, I TELL YOU!

V
3

VI

ONE NOON, MY DRUDGERY FINISHED, I WAS ABLE TO ATTEND AN IMPROMPTU GAME OF CARDS BETWEEN WOLF AND THE COOK...

WATCH OUT, CAPTAIN, I'M RIGHT 'ANDY AT "NAP"--BUT I ALSO KNOW 'OW TO LOSE WITH DIGNITY, LIKE A REAL GENTLEMAN!

I DON'T KNOW WHETHER WOLF LARSEN CHEATED, SOMETHING OF WHICH HE WAS PERFECTLY CAPABLE, BUT IN A FEW HOURS, THE COOK WAS CLEANED OUT...

MAMA! MY MONEY!

MUGRIDGE, GET OUT OF HERE, YOU HAVE WORK TO DO!

ONE HUNDRED AND EIGHTY-FIVE DOLLARS EVEN. JUST AS I THOUGHT. THE BEGGAR CAME ABOARD WITHOUT A CENT.

AND WHAT YOU HAVE WON IS MINE, SIR!

HUMP, I HAVE STUDIED SOME GRAMMAR IN MY TIME, AND I THINK YOUR TENSES ARE TANGLED. "WAS MINE," YOU SHOULD HAVE SAID, NOT "IS MINE."

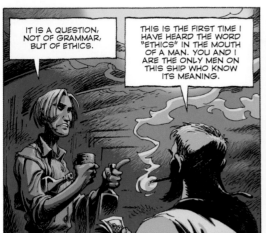

IT IS A QUESTION, NOT OF GRAMMAR, BUT OF ETHICS.

THIS IS THE FIRST TIME I HAVE HEARD THE WORD "ETHICS" IN THE MOUTH OF A MAN. YOU AND I ARE THE ONLY MEN ON THIS SHIP WHO KNOW ITS MEANING.

THEN YOU DON'T BELIEVE IN ALTRUISM?

YOU MEAN: HELPING PEOPLE OR SOMETHING OF THE SORT? OH, YES, I REMEMBER IT NOW. I RAN ACROSS IT IN SPENCER.

SPENCER! HAVE YOU READ HIM?

NOT VERY MUCH. I UNDERSTOOD QUITE A GOOD DEAL OF "FIRST PRINCIPLES," BUT HIS "BIOLOGY" TOOK THE WIND OUT OF MY SAILS, AND HIS "PSYCHOLOGY" LEFT ME IN THE DOLDRUMS FOR MANY A DAY.

DO YOU KNOW BROWNINGS'S POETRY?

I HAVE A VOLUME OF HIM IN MY CABIN AND I FIND THAT...

WE SPENT THREE DAYS DISCOURSING THUS, WOLF LARSEN HAVING RELIEVED ME OF MY DUTIES WITH MUGRIDGE, WHICH I FORESAW WOULD BRING ME TROUBLE.

VI
2

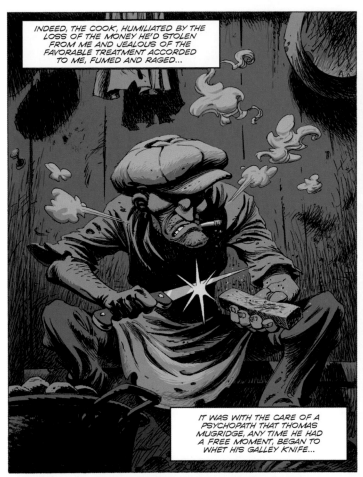

INDEED, THE COOK, HUMILIATED BY THE LOSS OF THE MONEY HE'D STOLEN FROM ME AND JEALOUS OF THE FAVORABLE TREATMENT ACCORDED TO ME, FUMED AND RAGED...

IT WAS WITH THE CARE OF A PSYCHOPATH THAT THOMAS MUGRIDGE, ANY TIME HE HAD A FREE MOMENT, BEGAN TO WHET HIS GALLEY KNIFE...

THE HIGHLY REFINED CREW HASTENED TO REASSURE ME ON THE DESTINATION OF THIS METICULOUS OCCUPATION...

HE MUST BE FIXING A DISH MADE FROM CHICKEN HEART, EH, HUMP? HA HA! HA!

IT GOT TO THE POINT THAT, WHENEVER I LEFT THE GALLEY, I WENT OUT BACKWARDS-- TO THE AMUSEMENT OF THE SAILORS AND HUNTERS...

VI
3

AT TIMES I THOUGHT OF THROWING MYSELF ON THE MERCY OF WOLF LARSEN, BUT WHAT HOPE OF PROTECTION WAS THERE FROM THE DEVIL?

?

PALAVERING WITH YOU NO LONGER AMUSES ME. YOUR WORDS HAVE NO WEIGHT. HOW CAN YOU HOLD FORTH ON YOUR IMMORTAL SOUL AND SOIL YOURSELF AT THE SIGHT OF A SHARP KNIFE IN A COOK'S HANDS?

COOKY CANNOT HURT YOU. HE CAN ONLY GIVE YOU A BOOST ON THE PATH YOU MUST ETERNALLY TREAD.

OR, IF YOU DO NOT WISH TO BE BOOSTED YET, WHY NOT BOOST COOKY? STICK A KNIFE IN HIM AND LET HIS SPIRIT FREE. AND WHO KNOWS? --IT MAY BE A VERY BEAUTIFUL SPIRIT THAT WILL GO SOARING UP.

BE ALTRUISTIC. OPEN THE DOOR OF LIFE ETERNAL TO HIM.

WITH A BIG KNIFE.

INCAPABLE OF CLOSING MY EYES, MY NERVES FRAYED, I WONDERED IF IT WEREN'T PREFERABLE TO SLIP INTO THE BLACK WATERS THAN TO END UP STABBED IN MY BERTH BY A MURDEROUS HAND, WHEN LOUIS APPROACHED ME...

I BELIEVE IN EQUAL CHANCES! THAT'LL COST YOU FIVE CANS OF CONDENSED MILK-- BUT HURRY UP AND PAY ME BEFORE HE GUTS YOU.

THE CONFRONTATION TOOK PLACE. EVEN TODAY, I STILL HAVE TROUBLE UNDERSTANDING HOW I, VAN WEYDEN, A CALM FELLOW, SON OF A GOOD FAMILY, HELD THE LIFE OF A MAN AT THE END OF MY BLADE, LIKE THE WORST SCOUNDREL...

THE ADRENALINE SHOT THAT ENSUED MADE ME TREMBLE LIKE A LEAF, BUT SUBSEQUENTLY, THIS CONTEMPTIBLE DEED EARNED ME THE CREW'S ESTEEM AND MUGRIDGE'S FEARFUL RESPECT...

HA! HA! HA! MAYBE YOU'LL FINALLY DO SOMETHING WITH YOUR LIFE! YOU'RE FINALLY STARTING TO WALK ON YOUR OWN.

VI
5

VII

I HAVE DISCOVERED WOLF LARSEN'S TORMENT. MY INTIMACY WITH HIM INCREASES, IF BY INTIMACY MAY BE DENOTED THOSE RELATIONS BETWEEN MASTER AND MAN, OR, BETTER YET, BETWEEN KING AND JESTER...

THIS DEVIL OF A MAN IS STRICKEN WITH BLINDING HEADACHES, AND HIS MUFFLED SOBS WOULD HAVE MADE ME FEEL SORRY FOR HIM, IF I DIDN'T HATE HIM SO MUCH; LIKE EVERYONE ON BOARD, MOREOVER.

THIS MORNING, HOWEVER, I FOUND HIM WELL AND HARD AT WORK...

I SAW HIM IN THE GLOOM OF HIS ROOM, HUDDLED, HIS HEAD BURIED IN HIS HANDS, FOR THREE DAYS AND THREE NIGHTS, SUFFERING WITHOUT PLAINT, ALONE, LIKE WILD ANIMALS SUFFER.

VII
1

HELLO, HUMP, I'M JUST FINISHING THE FINISHING TOUCHES.

BUT WHAT IS IT?

NAVIGATION REDUCED TO KINDERGARTEN SIMPLICITY. FROM TODAY A CHILD WILL BE ABLE TO NAVIGATE A SHIP. ⇥ARF! ARF! ARF!⇤

YOU MUST BE WELL UP IN MATHEMATICS. WHERE DID YOU GO TO SCHOOL?

NEVER SAW THE INSIDE OF ONE, WORSE LUCK! NEVERTHELESS I'LL BE ABLE TO REVEL IN PIGGISHNESS WITH ALL NIGHT IN WHILE OTHER MEN DO THE WORK.

ALSO, I HAVE ENJOYED WORKING IT OUT.

THE CREATIVE JOY...

⇥PFFF!⇤ THE JOY OF THE QUICK OVER THE DEAD, YOU MEAN! THE TRIUMPH OF MOVEMENT OVER MATTER, THE PRIDE OF THE YEAST! ⇥ARF! ARF! ARF!⇤

WOLF LARSEN PLUNGED ANEW INTO HIS CALCULATIONS WITH A STUDIOUS ATTENTION AND DELICACY THAT FORMED A CURIOUS CONTRAST WITH HIS CUSTOMARY BRUTALITY...

AT THAT INSTANT, CONCENTRATING AS HE WAS, THE LINES OF HIS NOSE, HIS MOUTH, HIS FOREHEAD EVOKED A SCULPTURE FROM ANTIQUITY, A HERO OF MYTHOLOGY...

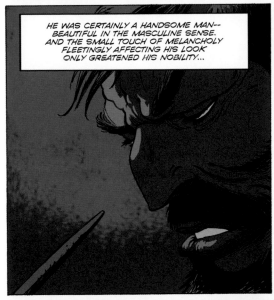

HE WAS CERTAINLY A HANDSOME MAN-- BEAUTIFUL IN THE MASCULINE SENSE. AND THE SMALL TOUCH OF MELANCHOLY FLEETINGLY AFFECTING HIS LOOK ONLY GREATENED HIS NOBILITY...

HOW COULD AN INDIVIDUAL OF SUCH POTENTIAL, OF SUCH POWER, HAVE ESCAPED ALL MORALITY? HE WAS NOT IMMORAL, BUT MERELY UNMORAL.

WHO WAS HE? WHAT WAS HE? MY CURIOSITY BURST FROM ME IN A FLOOD OF SPEECH...

DON'T YOU THINK, SOMETIMES, THAT YOU'VE WASTED YOUR LIFE?

VIII
3

WITH THE POWER THAT IS YOURS AND UNPOSSESSED OF MORAL INSTINCT, YOU MIGHT HAVE MASTERED A VASTER WORLD THAN THIS WALNUT SHELL!

AND TODAY, AT THE TOP OF YOUR LIFE, YOU LIVE A SORDID EXISTENCE AMONGST BRUTES, HUNTING SEA ANIMALS FOR THE SATISFACTION OF WOMAN'S VANITY! DID YOU LACK AMBITION?

HUMP, DO YOU KNOW THE PARABLE OF THE SOWER WHO WENT FORTH TO SOW?

IT MUST BE ADMITTED THAT IF MY SEED WERE A GOOD ONE, IT MUST HAVE SPRUNG UP IN AN UNFAVORABLE SETTING, AND NOBODY CAN RAISE HIMSELF HIGHER THAN HIS ROOTS ALLOW.

I WAS THE SON OF DANES BORN IN NORWEGIAN LANDS, AND MY PARENTS, PEASANTS OF THE SEA, LIKE THEIR ANCESTORS, SOWED THEIR SONS ON THE WAVES!

VII
4

FORTUNE HAD IT THAT, FROM ONE SHIP TO ANOTHER, BETWEEN THE BLOWS OF THE SKIPPERS AND THE SCORN OF THE CREWS, I DID IT ALL FOR MYSELF-- NAVIGATION, MATHEMATICS, SCIENCE, LITERATURE, AND WHAT NOT.

AND, HUMP, I CAN TELL YOU THAT YOU KNOW MORE ABOUT ME THAN ANY LIVING MAN, EXCEPT MY OWN BROTHER.

AND WHAT IS HE? WHERE IS HE?

MASTER OF THE STEAMSHIP MACEDONIA, SEAL-HUNTER. WE WILL MEET HIM MOST PROBABLY ON THE JAPAN COAST. MEN CALL HIM "DEATH" LARSEN.

DEATH LARSEN! IS HE LIKE YOU?

HA! HA! HA! HARDLY. HE'S HAPPY! THAT ILLITERATE IS TOO BUSY LIVING LIFE TO THINK ABOUT IT.

The GHOST

MY MISTAKE WAS IN EVER OPENING BOOKS.

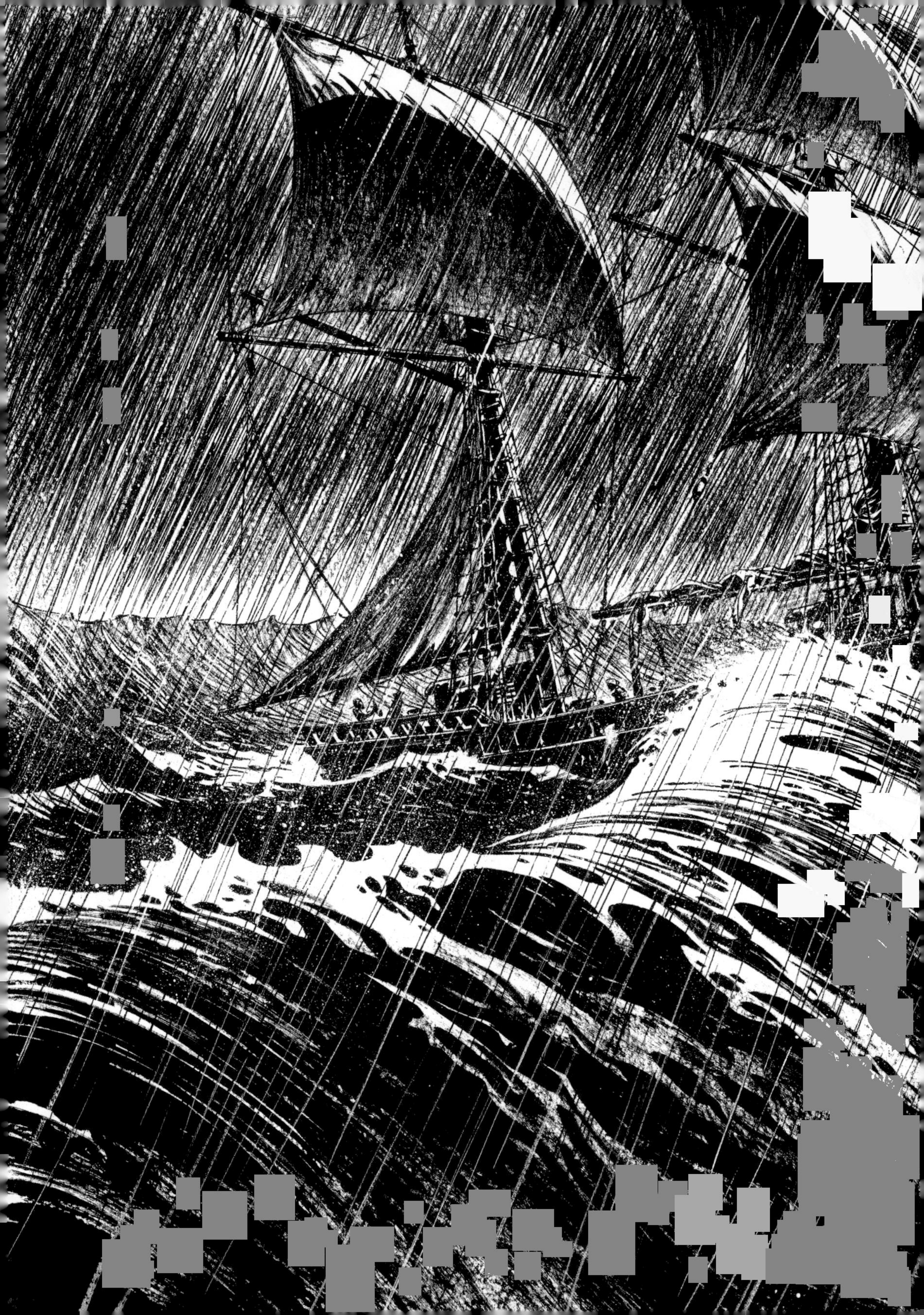

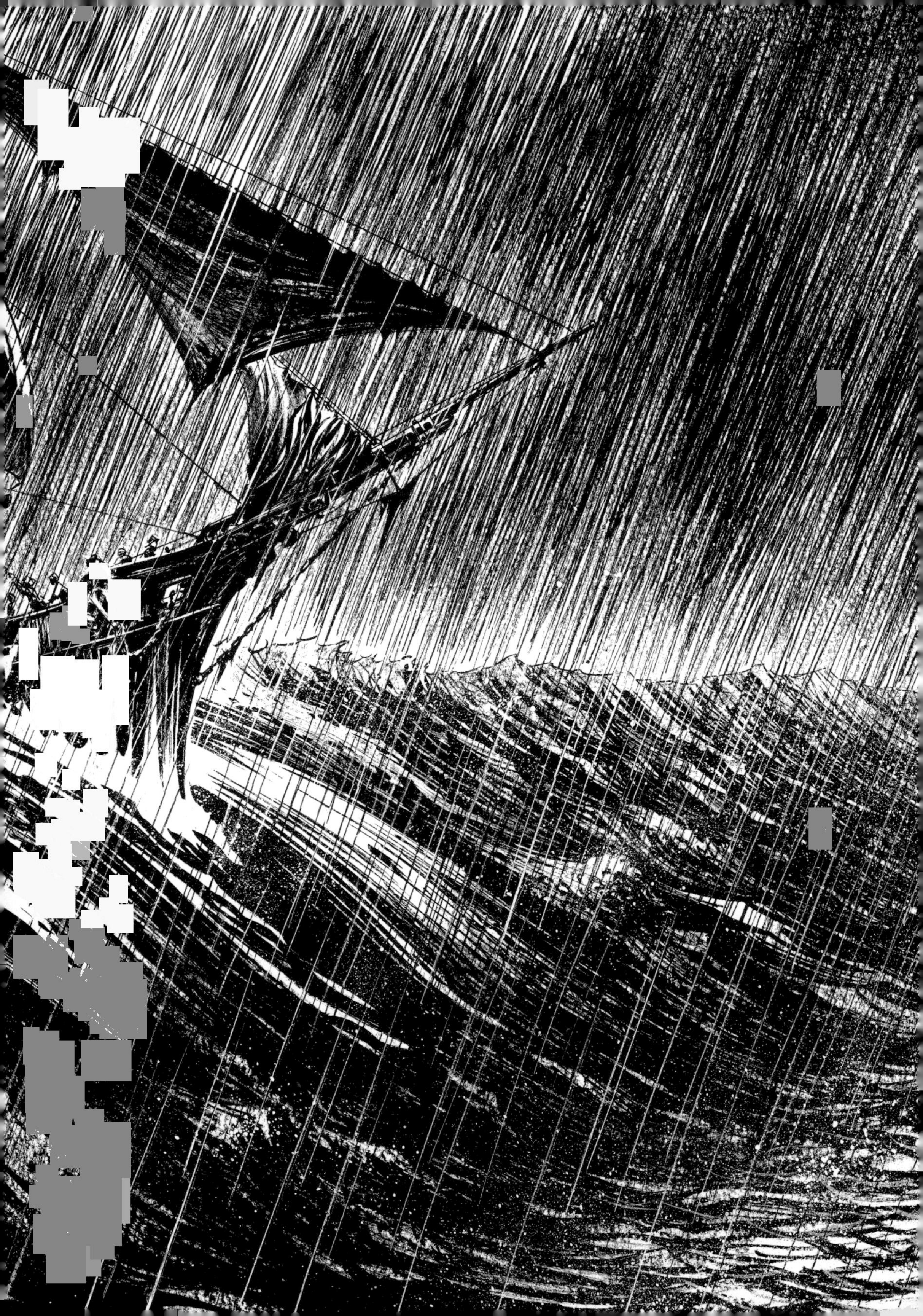

VIII

THE GHOST HAS ATTAINED THE SOUTHERNMOST POINT OF THE ARC SHE IS DESCRIBING ACROSS THE PACIFIC, AND IS ALREADY BEGINNING TO EDGE AWAY TO THE WEST AND NORTH TOWARD SOME LONE ISLAND, WHERE SHE WILL FILL HER WATER-CASKS BEFORE PROCEEDING TO THE SEASON'S HUNT...

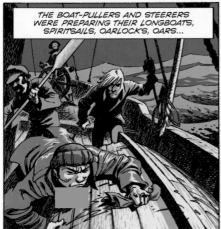

THE BOAT-PULLERS AND STEERERS WERE PREPARING THEIR LONGBOATS, SPIRITSAILS, OARLOCKS, OARS...

LOUIS HAS ALSO GIVEN ME ADDITIONAL INFORMATION ABOUT DEATH LARSEN...

WE MAY EXPECT TO MEET DEATH LARSEN ON THE JAPAN COAST. AND LOOK OUT FOR SQUALLS, FOR THEY HATE ONE ANOTHER LIKE THE WOLF WHELPS THEY ARE.

DEATH LARSEN IS IN COMMAND OF THE ONLY SEALING-STEAMER IN THE FLEET, THE MACEDONIA, WHICH CARRIES FOURTEEN BOATS, INSTEAD OF THE USUAL SIX. THERE IS WILD TALK OF CANNON ABOARD...

MY PHYSIQUE WAS TRANSFORMING. MY MUSCLES ARE INCREASING IN SIZE. MY HANDS, HOWEVER, ARE A SPECTACLE FOR GRIEF, AND I AM SUFFERING FROM BOILS, DUE TO THE DIET...

?

"WHAT, WITHOUT ASKING, HITHER HURRIED *WHENCE?* AND, WITHOUT ASKING, *WHITHER* HURRIED HENCE! OH, MANY A CUP OF THIS FORBIDDEN WINE MUST DROWN THE MEMORY OF THAT INSOLENCE!"

GREAT! "INSOLENCE"! HE COULD NOT HAVE USED A BETTER WORD!

YOU'RE READING THE "RUBAIYAT"?

I'VE THOUGHT MUCH ABOUT YOUR DREAM OF IMMORTALITY!

AND I THINK IT'S BOSH!

>GGLLL...<

WATCH HOW YOU FLAIL, HOW YOU CLUTCH MY ARM.

IF YOU WERE SO SURE OF YOUR EXISTENCE IN THE HEREAFTER, WOULD YOUR BODY BE CRYING, AS NOW: "TO *LIVE!* TO *LIVE!* TO *LIVE!*"?

G--

YOUR ARGUMENTS ARE TOO-- ER-- FORCIBLE.

YOU'LL BE ALL RIGHT IN HALF AN HOUR, AND I PROMISE YOU I WON'T USE ANY MORE PHYSICAL DEMONSTRATIONS.

VIII
3

IF WOLF LARSEN WAS RESPONSIBLE FOR ALL THE FEUDS, QUARRELS, AND GRUDGES POISONING RELATIONS ON BOARD, THOMAS MUGRIDGE ALSO PLAYED HIS PART...

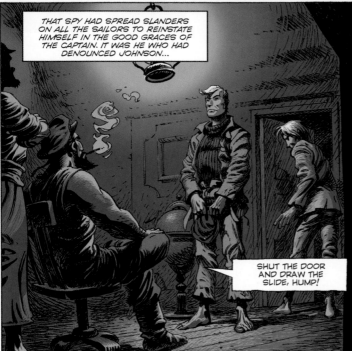

THAT SPY HAD SPREAD SLANDERS ON ALL THE SAILORS TO REINSTATE HIMSELF IN THE GOOD GRACES OF THE CAPTAIN. IT WAS HE WHO HAD DENOUNCED JOHNSON...

SHUT THE DOOR AND DRAW THE SLIDE, HUMP!

YONSON--

MY NAME IS JOHNSON, SIR.

WELL, JOHNSON, THEN, DAMN YOU! CAN YOU GUESS WHY I HAVE SENT FOR YOU?

YES, AND NO, SIR. MY WORK IS DONE WELL. SO THERE CANNOT BE ANY COMPLAINT.

VIII
4

AND THAT IS ALL?

I KNOW YOU HAVE IT IN FOR ME. YOU DO NOT LIKE ME BECAUSE I AM TOO MUCH OF A MAN.

YEAH-- I UNDERSTAND YOU'RE NOT QUITE SATISFIED WITH THOSE OILSKINS.

NO, I AM NOT. THEY ARE NO GOOD, SIR.

DO YOU KNOW WHAT HAPPENS TO MEN WHO SAY WHAT YOU'VE SAID ABOUT MY SLOP-CHEST AND ME?

I KNOW, SIR.

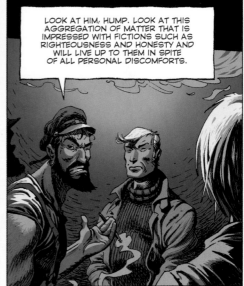

LOOK AT HIM, HUMP. LOOK AT THIS AGGREGATION OF MATTER THAT IS IMPRESSED WITH FICTIONS SUCH AS RIGHTEOUSNESS AND HONESTY AND WILL LIVE UP TO THEM IN SPITE OF ALL PERSONAL DISCOMFORTS.

I THINK THAT HE IS A BETTER MAN THAN YOU ARE. HIS HUMAN FICTIONS MADE FOR NOBILITY AND MANHOOD. COMPARED TO HIM, YOU ARE A PAUPER.

POSSIBLE, BUT IF THIS BIT OF THE FERMENT LOSES HIS LIFE, HIS IDEALS WILL BE LOST, TOO!

VIII 5

IN THE MEANTIME, I CAN BREAK THEM!

STAY, HUMP. WHAT DO YOU FEAR? IT'S ONLY THE FLEETING FORM WE MAY DEMOLISH!

THE FOLLOWING MINUTES SEEMED LIKE CENTURIES TO ME. THE CABIN WAS TRANSFORMED INTO AN ABATTOIR. EXHAUSTED FINALLY, THEY HOVE JOHNSON'S INERT BODY OUT ON DECK LIKE A SACK OF RUBBISH.

DAMN YOUR SOUL, WOLF LARSEN! MURDERER! YOU PIG!

WHY DON'T YOU COME KILL ME? DAMN SIGHT BETTER DEAD THAN IN YOUR CLUTCHES! KILL ME! KILL ME!

VIII
6

SUCH LANGWIDGE! SHOCKIN'!

FILTHY ROACH! YOU DESERVE THIS!

OH, LORD! 'ELP! 'ELP! ~ARGH!~

HA HA HA HA HA HA HA HA HA HA HA HA

I CONFESS THAT I DELIGHTED IN THIS BEATING LEACH WAS GIVING TO THOMAS MUGRIDGE...

BY HALING FORTH WOLF LARSEN'S SOUL NAKED TO THE SCORN OF THE WHOLE CREW, HE'D DEMONSTRATED A TERRIBLE AUDACITY OF SUICIDAL COURAGE! WOLF LARSEN SEEMED LOST IN A GREAT CURIOSITY. WAS HE OBSERVING THIS WILD STIRRING OF YEASTY LIFE OR CONTEMPLATING HIS VENGEANCE?

ALL I KNOW IS THAT MY POWERLESSNESS BEFORE THE CAPTAIN, MY POWERLESSNESS TO HELP JOHNSON BORE A NAME: COWARDICE!

LEACH BANDAGED JOHNSON; MUGRIDGE LICKED HIS WOUNDS BY HIMSELF; AND THE DEVIL, UNDERGOING ANOTHER BAD MIGRAINE ATTACK, WITHDREW INTO THE DEPTHS OF HIS DEN.

IX

IT WAS A CALM NIGHT. WE WERE OUT OF THE TRADES, AND THE GHOST WAS FORGING AHEAD SLOWLY...

IT HAS DAWNED UPON ME THAT I HAVE NEVER PLACED A PROPER VALUATION UPON WOMANKIND.

AND HOW WELCOME WOULD HAVE BEEN THE FEEL OF THE SWEET PRESENCE OF MY MOTHER AND SISTERS WHO I USUALLY DEEMED TO BE SO INTRUSIVE...

AND ALSO HOW, IN THE ABSENCE OF WOMEN, THE MEN SURROUNDING ME, ABANDONED TO THEMSELVES, FELL INTO COARSENESS AND SAVAGERY...

IT WAS TOO STUFFY TO SLEEP BELOW. I LEFT MY CABIN, TUCKED MY BLANKET UNDER MY ARM AND WENT UP ON DECK TO SLEEP THERE.

IX
1

AS I PASSED BY HARRISON, I STARTED UP A SHORT CONVERSATION WITH HIM...

TAKING A FRESH HOLD OF MY BEDCLOTHES TO START ON, WHEN MOVEMENT CAUGHT MY EYE ASTERN.

WHERE'S THE MATE?

I DON'T KNOW, SIR. I SAW HIM GO FOR'ARD A LITTLE WHILE AGO.

SO DID I GO FOR'ARD. BUT YOU WILL OBSERVE THAT I DIDN'T COME BACK THE WAY I WENT. CAN YOU EXPLAIN IT?

YOU MUST HAVE BEEN OVERBOARD, SIR!

SHALL I LOOK FOR HIM IN THE STEERAGE, SIR?

YOU WON'T FIND HIM, HUMP. HE MUST BE FAR AWAY AND DEEP! NEVER MIND YOUR BEDDING. COME ON.

YOUR SCALP IS LAID OPEN, DO YOU WANT ME TO BANDAGE YOU?

QUIET!

IT WAS MY FIRST DESCENT INTO THE FORECASTLE, AND I SHALL NOT SOON FORGET MY IMPRESSION OF IT...

THIS WAS EVIDENTLY WOLF LARSEN'S QUEST-- TO FIND THE MEN WHO WEREN'T TRULY SLEEPING.

SUDDENLY THE LIGHT WAS DASHED FROM THE CAPTAIN'S HAND AND THE FORECASTLE LEFT IN DARKNESS...

WE GOT HIM!

GET A KNIFE, SOMEBODY!

IT WAS CLEARLY LEACH'S VOICE, BUT JOHNSON AND THEIR MATES LEAPT UPON WOLF LARSEN...

THE FEARSOME SOUND OF AN UNEQUAL BATTLE PITTING A PACK OF DOGS AGAINST A WOLF WAS SOON REPLACED BY THE CRASHING ABOUT OF THE ENTWINED BODIES, THE LABORED BREATHING, AND THE SHORT, QUICK GASPS OF SUDDEN PAIN...

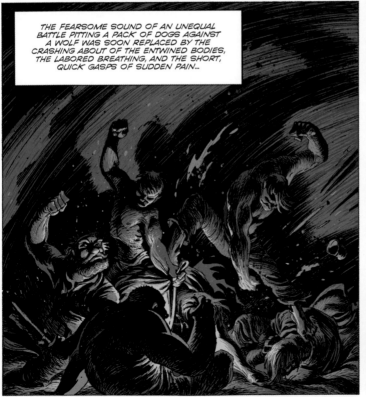

I MANAGED TO CRAWL INTO AN EMPTY BUNK OUT OF THE WAY...

IX
5

WOLF LARSEN, DOWN AT THE VERY FIRST, REGAINED THE UPPER HAND. NO MAN, UNLESS IT WERE HERCULES IN PERSON, COULD HAVE ACCOMPLISHED SUCH A FEAT OF STRENGTH.

WON'T SOMEBODY GET A KNIFE?!

HE'D REACHED THE SAVING LADDER AND BEGUN HIS ASCENT.

SLAM

X

SOMEBODY STRIKE A LIGHT.

MY THUMB'S OUT OF JOINT.

SEEING HOW MY FINGERS FEEL, I MUST HAVE BROKEN HIS JAW!

SO IT WAS YOU, YOU BLACK BEGGAR? YOU'LL PAY FOR THAT.

G'WAN, YOU KELLY. HOW IN HELL DID HE KNOW IT WAS YOU IN THE DARK?

HOW DID HE GET AWAY?

BECAUSE HE IS THE DEVIL! AND NOT ONE OF YOU TO GET A KNIFE!

HOW'LL HE KNOW WHICH WAS WHICH? UNLESS ONE OF US PEACHES.

HE'LL KNOW AS SOON AS EVER HE CLAPS EYES ON US. WE'RE DONE FOR.

A NICE LOT OF GAZABAS YOU ARE! IF YOU TALKED LESS WITH YER MOUTH AND DID SOMETHING WITH YER HANDS, HE'D-A-BEN DONE WITH BY NOW. A-BEEFIN' AND BELLERIN' 'ROUND, AS THOUGH HE'D KILL YOU ALL. HE CAN'T AFFORD TO. HOW'D HE RUN THE SHIP?

DON'T BE AFRAID. IT'S ME AND JOHNSON WHO HAVE TO FACE THE MUSIC! SO SHUT YER FACES. I WANT TO GET SOME SLEEP.

I'M COMING!

HUMP! THE OLD MAN WANTS YOU!

?

?

HE AIN'T DOWN HERE!

NO YOU DON'T! YOU DAMN LITTLE SNEAK!

LET HIM GO, KELLY. I TELL YER, HE'S ALL RIGHT. HE DON'T LIKE THE OLD MAN NO MORE THAN YOU OR ME.

COME, GET TO WORK, DOCTOR. THE SIGNS ARE FAVORABLE FOR AN EXTENSIVE PRACTICE THIS VOYAGE.

I HAD NEVER BEFORE SEEN HIM STRIPPED, AND THE SIGHT OF HIS BODY QUITE TOOK MY BREATH AWAY. THE HEAD OF A BABYLONIAN KING ON THE BODY OF A TITAN...

AS HE MOVED ABOUT, THE GREAT MUSCLES LEAPT AND MOVED UNDER THE SATINY SKIN. I WAS AS STRONGLY IMPRESSED AS IF I'D SEEN THE ENGINES OF A GREAT BATTLESHIP.

GOD MADE YOU WELL.

YOU THINK? GOD HAS NOTHING TO DO WITH IT, BUT I SUPPOSE NATURE MADE ME TO GRIP, AND TEAR, AND DOMINATE.

WHAT A LACK OF GRANDEUR!

HA! HA!

I WAS SURPRISED, CONSIDERING THE FIERCE STRUGGLE IN THE FORECASTLE, AT THE SUPERFICIALITY OF HIS HURTS. THE MOST DELICATE WAS TO SEW UP THE WOUND ON HIS SCALP, WHICH HE'D RECEIVED BEFORE GOING OVERBOARD.

YOU ARE A HANDY MAN. YOU'LL TAKE THE PLACE OF THE NEWLY VACANT MATE.

I--I DON'T UNDERSTAND NAVIGATION, YOU KNOW. I REALLY DO NOT CARE TO SIT IN THE HIGH PLACES, I FIND LIFE PRECARIOUS ENOUGH IN MY PRESENT HUMBLE SITUATION. MEDIOCRITY HAS ITS COMPENSATIONS.

YOU KNOW FULL WELL IT'S NOT A PROPOSITION, MR. VAN WEYDEN.

XI

NO MORE DISHES, CLEANING, OR POTATOES TO PEEL! THAT WAS THE FUNDAMENTAL ADVANTAGE OF MY NEW DUTIES...

IGNORANT OF THE SIMPLEST DUTIES OF MATE, I WOULD HAVE FARED BADLY HAD THE SAILORS NOT SYMPATHIZED WITH ME. WOLF LARSEN HIMSELF SILENCED THE JUSTIFIED SARCASM OF THE HUNTERS TOWARDS ME...

DESPITE THE DARK PROSPECT OF THE COMING DAYS, THOSE DAYS OF LEARNING NAVIGATION WERE MY PLEASANTEST HOURS ON THE GHOST...

YOU'RE NO LONGER STANDING ON YOUR LATE FATHER'S LEGS. NOW YOU CAN GET PAID FOR PILOTING ANY COASTAL SCHOONER.

MAYBE ONE DAY YOU'LL STOP CRITIQUING OTHERS' BOOKS AND TAKE THE RISK OF WRITING YOUR OWN!

UNLESS I KILL YOU FIRST, OF COURSE! HA! HA! HA!

YOU'RE TRULY A GOOD-FOR-
NOTHING IRISHMAN, LEACH!
RETURN TO YOUR POST INSTEAD
OF STANDING THERE!

WHY DON'T YOU MAKE AN END OF IT WITH
LEACH AND JOHNSON? YOU DEVOTE YOURSELF
MORNING, NOON, AND NIGHT, TO MAKING
LIFE UNLIVABLE FOR THEM. AH, BUT IT IS
COWARDLY! YOU HAVE ALL THE ADVANTAGE!

PERHAPS I SHOULD LISTEN TO YOU, FOR YOU'RE A SPECIALIST IN THAT DOMAIN.

THE SITUATION REVOLTS YOU AND YOU DON'T REVOLT! IF YOU WERE REALLY GREAT, YOU'D JOIN FORCES WITH LEACH AND JOHNSON. BUT YOU ARE AFRAID. YOU WANT TO LIVE, NO MATTER WHAT THE COST.

YOU LIVE IGNOMINIOUSLY, UNTRUE TO THE BEST YOU DREAM OF, SINNING AGAINST YOUR WHOLE PITIFUL LITTLE CODE.

I WILL LISTEN TO YOU NO LONGER. FOR I INTEND TO REMAIN SINCERE TO THE PROMPTINGS OF MY LIFE.

THE FOLLOWING NIGHT, DURING THE CAPTAIN'S SLEEP, I WENT TO FIND JOHNSON AND LEACH WHO SOOTHED THE WOUNDS OF THOSE COMMENTS SOMEWHAT...

WHAT DO YOU THINK YOU CAN CHANGE, MR. VAN WEYDEN? WE'RE DEAD MEN, WE'RE NOT FOOLING OURSELVES.

IF IT'S YER LUCK TO EVER MAKE 'FRISCO ONCE MORE, WILL YOU HUNT UP MATT McCARTHY? HE'S MY OLD MAN. TELL HIM I LIVED TO BE SORRY FOR THE TROUBLE I BROUGHT HIM AND THE THINGS I DONE, AND-- AND JUST TELL "GOD BLESS HIM," FOR ME.

HARRISON AND KELLY MADE AN ATTEMPT TO ESCAPE WHILE FILLING OUR WATER-BARRELS ON WAINWRIGHT ISLAND...

XI
3

85

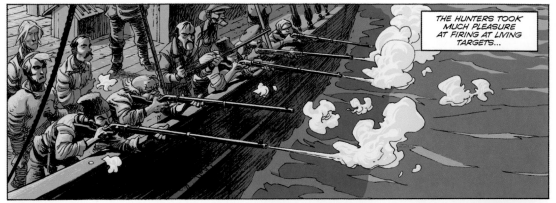

THE HUNTERS TOOK MUCH PLEASURE AT FIRING AT LIVING TARGETS...

THE TWO WRETCHES, RECAPTURED, NOW WANDER LISTLESSLY ON BOARD, LIKE THE LIVING DEAD AWAITING THEIR PUNISHMENT...

WE RAISED THE COAST OF JAPAN AND PICKED UP WITH THE GREAT SEAL HERD....

BLAM

BLAM

BLAM

IT WAS ONLY AT THAT INSTANT THAT I REALIZED HOW MUCH THE CREW AND HUNTERS, SINCE THE BEGINNING OF THE TRIP, HAD STRAINED TOWARDS THIS GOAL: EXTRACTING THEIR SALARY FROM THE SEA; A GOLD RUSH, WITH THEIR NOSES IN GUNPOWDER AND THEIR FEET IN GUTS.

XI
4

ACCOMPLISHED PREDATORS, WE FOLLOWED THE HERD AND, EVERY DAY, WE SACRIFICED A MAXIMUM OF ANIMALS IN HONOR OF THE FASHION GODDESS. NO MAN ATE OF THE SEAL MEAT. ONCE THE SKINS WERE SALTED DOWN, WE FLUNG THE CARCASSES TO THE SHARKS...

AFTER A GOOD DAY'S KILLING, THE GHOST'S DECKS RAN RED. THE MEN, LIKE BUTCHERS, REMOVED THE SKINS FROM THE PRETTY SEA-CREATURES...

MY STOMACH REVOLTED, IT WAS MY TASK TO TALLY THE PELTS.

THEN, THERE WAS ONE BEAUTIFUL DAY, WHEN THE SIX BOATS HAD GONE SO FAR AWAY THAT THE REPORTS OF THE GUNS REACHED US ONLY WEAKLY...

THE WIND HAD DIED, AND THE BAROMETER STARTED DROPPING.

IT'S NO SQUALL, HUMP. OLD MOTHER NATURE'S GOING TO GET UP ON HER HIND LEGS AND HOWL FOR ALL THAT'S IN HER. THIS WON'T BE LITERATURE! HA! HA! HA!

XI
5

THE SUN HAD DIMMED AT TWO IN THE AFTERNOON. A WHISPER OF WIND MADE THE CANVAS FLAP. THE GHOST AWOKE AND THE SEA STARTED TO RISE...

THERE WERE ONLY THREE OF US TO STEER THE SCHOONER DURING THE HUNT. MY ROLE AT THAT MOMENT WAS TO BE IN THE FORE CROSSTREE TO SCAN THE HORIZON AND RAISE THE BOATS BEFORE THE STORM ENGULFED THEM...

INDEED, AS I GAZED AT THE HEAVY SEA THROUGH WHICH WE WERE RUNNING, I DOUBTED THAT THERE WAS A BOAT AFLOAT.

THE SCHOONER WOULD LIFT AND SEND ACROSS SOME GREAT WAVE, BURYING HER STARBOARD RAIL FROM VIEW, AND COVERING HER DECK TO THE HATCHES WITH THE BOILING OCEAN, FORCING MUGRIDGE, POSTED TO THE MANEUVERS OF THE FORE-SHEET, TO TAKE SHELTER IN THE SHROUDS...

FOR AN HOUR, I CLUNG TO THE INVERTED PENDULUM, SEEING NOTHING BUT A CHAIN OF LIVING, BOILING MOUNTAINS. THEN, WAY OVER THERE, BRIEFLY, A TINY POINT OF BLACK...

XI
6

OBEYING WOLF LARSEN'S ORDERS, I WAS NOW BACK DOWN ON THE DECK AND I COULD MAKE OUT PLAINLY THE BOAT AGAINST THE WAVE AND THE THREE MEN FRANTICALLY BAILING...

EACH TIME THAT SHE REAPPEARED WAS A MIRACLE...

WOLF LARSEN HOVE TO AND PANDEMONIUM BROKE LOOSE...

IT SEEMED THAT THE END OF EVERYTHING HAD COME. ON ALL SIDES THERE WAS A RENDING AND CRASHING OF WOOD AND STEEL AND CANVAS. THE GHOST WAS BEING TORN TO FRAGMENTS...

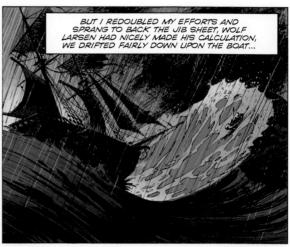

BUT I REDOUBLED MY EFFORTS AND SPRANG TO BACK THE JIB SHEET, WOLF LARSEN HAD NICELY MADE HIS CALCULATION, WE DRIFTED FAIRLY DOWN UPON THE BOAT...

HOISTING THE BOAT IS MORE DIFFICULT TO EXECUTE THAN WRITE ABOUT, MEANWHILE KERFOOT, OOFTY-OOFTY, AND KELLY LEAPT ABOARD...

KERFOOT'S MIDDLE FINGER WAS CRUSHED BUT, WITHOUT THE SLIGHTEST COMPLAINT, HE HELPED US LASH THE BOAT IN ITS PLACE...

AND THE SHIP RESUMED ITS COURSE BY FILLING ITS SAILS...

A HALF-HOUR LATER, IN THE SAME CONDITIONS, WE RECOVERED JOCK HORNER, FAT LOUIS, AND JOHNSON...

WOLF LARSEN, HIS HANDS GRIPPING THE SPOKES AND HOLDING TO THE SCHOONER TO THE COURSE OF HIS WILL, HIMSELF AN EARTH-GOD, DICTATED HIS LAW TO THE CATACLYSMIC QUAKES OF THE UNIVERSE...

THE GHOST *KICKED* LIKE A MADDENED HORSE AND WE, AS BRAVE AS ANTS IN A WASHTUB, WERE ONLY THERE TO SERVE IT.

XI
9

BY THE LAST LIGHT OF DAY, WE SIGHTED A THIRD BOAT. THE NUMBER FOUR, IT WAS UPSIDE DOWN AND THERE WAS NO HOPE FOR ITS OCCUPANTS..

THE CAPTAIN OBSTINATELY INSISTED ON RECOVERING THE BOAT. USELESS AND CRIMINAL EFFORTS, FOR THE BOAT SMASHED AGAINST THE HULL OF THE GHOST, AND KELLY WAS ENGULFED BY A WAVE...

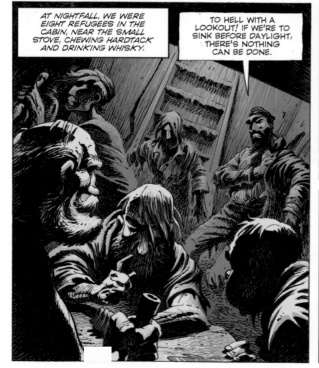

AT NIGHTFALL, WE WERE EIGHT REFUGEES IN THE CABIN, NEAR THE SMALL STOVE, CHEWING HARDTACK AND DRINKING WHISKY.

TO HELL WITH A LOOKOUT! IF WE'RE TO SINK BEFORE DAYLIGHT, THERE'S NOTHING CAN BE DONE.

I DON'T THINK IT WAS WORTH IT, A BROKEN BOAT FOR KELLY'S LIFE.

BUT KELLY DIDN'T AMOUNT TO MUCH. GOOD NIGHT.

XI
10

XII

THE NEXT DAY, WHILE THE SAILORS MADE REPAIRS, THE GHOST CRUISED BACK AND FORTH. WE SIGHTED OTHER SEALING SCHOONERS, MOST OF WHICH WERE IN SEARCH OF LOST BOATS...

TWO OF OUR BOATS WE TOOK OFF THE CISCO, AND TO WOLF'S LARSEN'S HUGE DELIGHT AND MY OWN GRIEF, HE CULLED SMOKE, WITH NILSON AND LEACH, FROM THE SAN DIEGO.

WE FOUND OURSELVES SHORT OF FOUR MEN AND WERE ONCE MORE HUNTING ON THE FLANK'S OF THE HERD.

THAT NIGHT, I WAS STILL TALLYING THE SKINS WHEN LEACH APPROACHED ME...

CAN YOU TELL ME, MR. VAN WEYDEN, HOW FAR WE ARE OFF THE COAST, AND WHAT THE BEARINGS OF YOKOHAMA ARE?

WEST-NORTHWEST AND FIVE HUNDRED MILES AWAY.

THANK YOU, SIR.

NEXT MORNING, NO. 3 BOAT AND JOHNSON AND LEACH WERE MISSING. WOLF LARSEN WAS FURIOUS. HE TOOK COMMAND AND DIRECTED THE PURSUIT, THE FOG HAVING DISAPPEARED.

IT WAS LOOKING FOR A NEEDLE IN A HAYSTACK, BUT ON THE MORNING OF THE THIRD DAY, A CRY CAME DOWN THAT THE BOAT WAS SIGHTED.

WOLF LARSEN'S TRIUMPHANT, SADISTIC SMILE LIT AN IRRESISTIBLE RAGE WITHIN ME. IT WAS FROM THE STEERAGE, A LOADED SHOT-GUN IN MY HANDS, WHEN I HEARD THE STARTLED CRY:

THERE'S FIVE MEN IN THAT BOAT!

FIVE?!

XII
2

TALK OF A MESS! HEE HEE HEE!

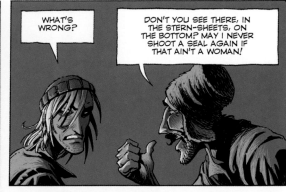

WHAT'S WRONG?

DON'T YOU SEE THERE, IN THE STERN-SHEETS, ON THE BOTTOM? MAY I NEVER SHOOT A SEAL AGAIN IF THAT AIN'T A WOMAN!

SHE SEEMED LIKE A BEING FROM ANOTHER WORLD.

MR. VAN WEYDEN! WILL YOU TAKE THE LADY TO THE SPARE PORT CABIN? SEE TO HER COMFORT.

NO NEED TO GO TO ANY GREAT TROUBLE!

WE SHOULD ARRIVE IN JAPAN BY DAY'S END. YOUR SHIP WILL TAKE US STRAIGHT THERE, WON'T IT?

XII
3

 IF IT WERE ANY OTHER CAPTAIN EXCEPT OURS I SHOULD SAY SO, BUT OUR CAPTAIN IS A STRANGE MAN, AND I BEG YOU TO BE PREPARED FOR ANYTHING. I WISH MERELY TO PREPARE YOU FOR THE WORST.

 I--I CONFESS I HARDLY DO UNDERSTAND. OR IS IT A MISCONCEPTION OF MINE THAT SHIPWRECKED PEOPLE ARE ALWAYS SHOWN EVERY CONSIDERATION? WE ARE SO CLOSE TO LAND.

 UM! LET'S JUST SAY YOU'VE STEPPED INTO A DARK TALE AND THAT OUR CAPTAIN PLAYS THE ROLE OF THE OGRE IN IT-- TO PERFECTION.

OH, I SEE, I'LL START BY GETTING SOME REST.

 I WAS SO TROUBLED I HAD QUITE FORGOTTEN THE EXISTENCE OF LEACH AND JOHNSON, WHEN SUDDENLY, LIKE A THUNDERCLAP--

BOAT HO!

XII
4

ALL HANDS WERE ON DECK AND A SERIOUS GUST OF WIND WAS SHAPING UP.

THREE OILERS AND A FOURTH ENGINEER! BUT WE'LL MAKE BOAT-PULLERS OUT OF THEM AT ANY RATE. NOW, WHAT OF THE LADY?

WHAT'S HER NAME, THEN?

I DON'T KNOW. SHE WAS VERY TIRED. WHAT VESSEL WAS IT?

MAIL STEAMER, THE CITY OF TOKIO, AN OLD TUB THAT FOUNDERED IN THAT TYPHOON.

AND YOU DON'T EVEN KNOW WHETHER SHE'S A MAID, WIFE OR WIDOW?

ARE YOU PLANNING TO TAKE THEM TO YOKOHAMA?

NO!

SET THE HELM INTO THE WIND!

WE INCREASED OUR LEAD, AND WHEN THE BOAT HAD DROPPED ASTERN SEVERAL MILES, WE HOVE TO AND WAITED.

THE BOAT DREW CLOSER AND CLOSER TO US. DEATH WAS STALKING THEM. THE SEA, PATIENT, WAS SLOWLY ABSORBING THEM.

THEY WERE A STONE'S THROW AWAY WHEN WOLF LARSEN HAD THE SCHOONER SPRING AWAY AGAIN.

THE MANEUVER WAS RENEWED TWO MORE TIMES, THEN A WAVE NO WORSE THAN ANY OTHER ERASED THEM, AND JOHNSON AND LEACH LEFT THIS VALE OF TEARS.

GOOD GOD! SIR, WHAT KIND OF CRAFT IS THIS?

YOU HAVE EYES, YOU HAVE SEEN.

XIII

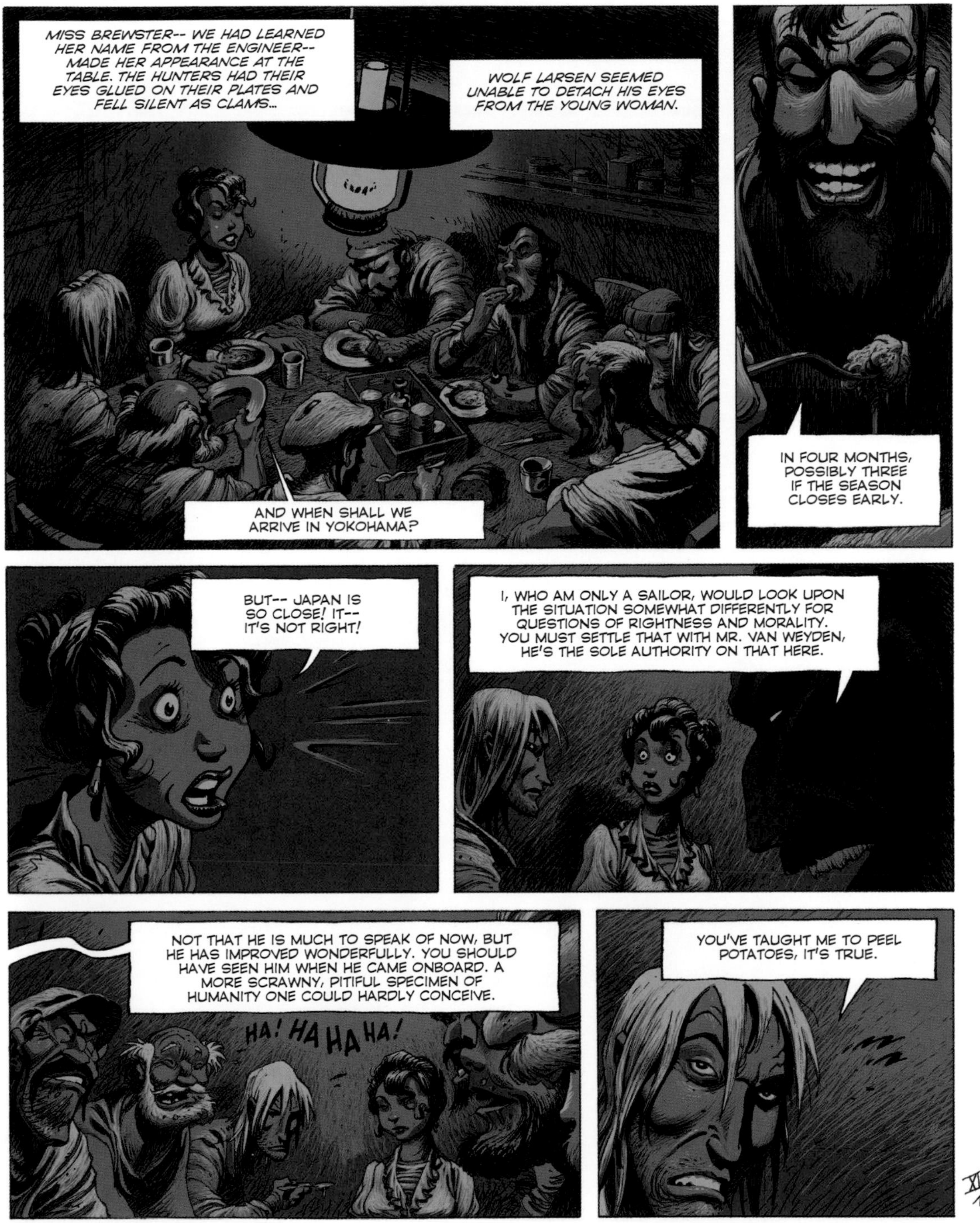
MISS BREWSTER-- WE HAD LEARNED HER NAME FROM THE ENGINEER-- MADE HER APPEARANCE AT THE TABLE. THE HUNTERS HAD THEIR EYES GLUED ON THEIR PLATES AND FELL SILENT AS CLAMS...
WOLF LARSEN SEEMED UNABLE TO DETACH HIS EYES FROM THE YOUNG WOMAN.
AND WHEN SHALL WE ARRIVE IN YOKOHAMA?
IN FOUR MONTHS, POSSIBLY THREE IF THE SEASON CLOSES EARLY.
BUT-- JAPAN IS SO CLOSE! IT-- IT'S NOT RIGHT!
I, WHO AM ONLY A SAILOR, WOULD LOOK UPON THE SITUATION SOMEWHAT DIFFERENTLY FOR QUESTIONS OF RIGHTNESS AND MORALITY. YOU MUST SETTLE THAT WITH MR. VAN WEYDEN, HE'S THE SOLE AUTHORITY ON THAT HERE.
NOT THAT HE IS MUCH TO SPEAK OF NOW, BUT HE HAS IMPROVED WONDERFULLY. YOU SHOULD HAVE SEEN HIM WHEN HE CAME ONBOARD. A MORE SCRAWNY, PITIFUL SPECIMEN OF HUMANITY ONE COULD HARDLY CONCEIVE.
HA! HA HA HA HA!
YOU'VE TAUGHT ME TO PEEL POTATOES, IT'S TRUE.

XIII
1

BY THE WAY, WHAT DO YOU DO FOR A LIVING? IF IT MEANS ANYTHING TO YOU, HAVE YOU EVER EARNED A DOLLAR BY YOUR OWN LABOR?

WHY CERTAINLY, I MUST HAVE EARNED A DOLLAR WHEN I LOST MY FIRST TOOTH.

BUT THAT WAS LONG AGO. AT PRESENT, HOWEVER, I EARN ABOUT EIGHTEEN HUNDRED DOLLARS A YEAR.

WHAT COMMODITIES DO YOU TURN OUT? WHAT TOOLS AND MATERIAL DO YOU REQUIRE?

PAPER AND INK, AND OH! ALSO A TYPEWRITER.

THEN, YOU ARE MAUD BREWSTER!

HOW-- HOW DO YOU KNOW?!

I REMEMBER WRITING A REVIEW OF A THIN LITTLE VOLUME--

YOU! YOU ARE *HUMPHREY VAN WEYDEN?* THE RENOWNED CRITIC?

I REMEMBER THAT TOO, TOO FLATTERING REVIEW.

NOT AT ALL! BESIDES, ALL MY BROTHER CRITICS WERE WITH ME. DIDN'T LANG INCLUDE YOUR "KISS ENDURED" AMONG THE FOUR SUPREME SONNETS BY WOMEN IN THE ENGLISH LANGUAGE?

THAT'S VERY FLATTERING! BUT EXCUSE ME, I DON'T UNDERSTAND. WE SURELY ARE NOT TO EXPECT SOME SEA-STORY FROM YOUR SOBER PEN?

NO, I AM NOT GATHERING MATERIAL, I ASSURE YOU. I HAVE NEITHER APTITUDE NOR INCLINATION FOR FICTION.

GO, GO, I PRAY YOU. DON'T MIND US! WE UNDERLINGS HAVE A LOT ON OUR PLATE, THAT'S ALL! WORK-- IF YOU KNOW WHAT I MEAN.

XIII
3

WOLF LARSEN, CHAGRINED BY THE TURN OF THE CONVERSATION AT THE TABLE, WAS LOOKING FOR AN OUTLET, AND ONCE AGAIN, IT FELL TO THOMAS MUGRIDGE TO BE THE VICTIM...

I WATCHED YOU SERVING. YOUR SHIRT IS FILTHY. YOU SMELL AS RANCID AS YOUR GALLEY. A LITTLE BATH WOULD DO YOU GOOD.

MERCY! I SWEAR TO YE, ME APRON'S CLEAN!

HA HA HA HA HA HA HA

I JUST WASHED IIIITTTT!

IT WAS A PITIFUL SPECTACLE. MUGRIDGE, DEPENDING ON THE TRACTION OF THE GHOST SOMETIMES EMERGED GASPING FOR BREATH, SOMETIMES SUBMERGED, SUFFERING ALL THE AGONIES OF HALF-DROWNING.

WHAT IS THE CAUSE OF THE MERRIMENT? ARE YOU FISHING?

I BEG YOU, COME NO CLOSER!

SHARK HO, SIR!

XIII
4

104

HEAVE IN! LIVELY! ALL HANDS TAIL ON!

AAAAAAAH

THIS GAME IS ORDINARILY WITHOUT CONSEQUENCES. THE SHARK WAS NOT IN THE RECKONING!

MR. VAN WEYDEN, WOULD YOU SEE AFTER THE WOUNDED MAN?

WHILE I MADE MUGRIDGE A TOURNIQUET, WOLF LARSEN HAD ALREADY CAUGHT THE SHARK WITH THE HELP OF A SWIVEL-HOOK BAITED WITH FAT SALT-PORK...

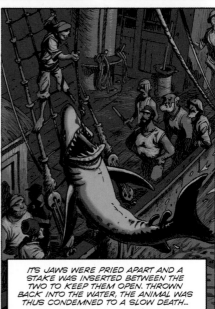

ITS JAWS WERE PRIED APART AND A STAKE WAS INSERTED BETWEEN THE TWO TO KEEP THEM OPEN. THROWN BACK INTO THE WATER, THE ANIMAL WAS THUS CONDEMNED TO A SLOW DEATH...

IT'S MONSTROUS! WHY DO YOU LET THIS HAPPEN?

MISS BREWSTER, WAIT!

XIII
5

I CAN DO NOTHING AGAINST WOLF LARSEN! I AM NOT OF A STATURE TO COMBAT HIM.

YESTERDAY, TOO, HE DELIBERATELY LET TWO MEN DROWN. TWO SAILORS MUCH STRONGER AND BRAVER THAN I, WHO DID THEIR ALL AGAINST HIM.

I'VE DREAMT A THOUSAND TIMES OF HIS DEATH, BUT CANNOT STEEL MYSELF TO KILL HIM. DO YOU UNDERSTAND, MAUD?

WHAT CAN WE DO THEN?

BE PATIENT, MAUD, AND WHEN THE TIME COMES, IF YOU AGREE, OBEY ME BLINDLY.

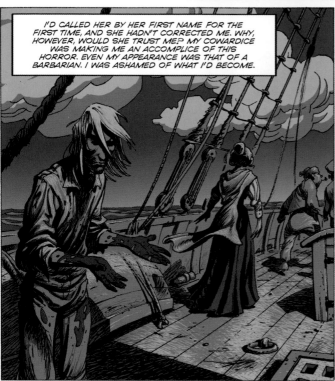

I'D CALLED HER BY HER FIRST NAME FOR THE FIRST TIME, AND SHE HADN'T CORRECTED ME. WHY, HOWEVER, WOULD SHE TRUST ME? MY COWARDICE WAS MAKING ME AN ACCOMPLICE OF THIS HORROR. EVEN MY APPEARANCE WAS THAT OF A BARBARIAN. I WAS ASHAMED OF WHAT I'D BECOME.

WE SAILED FOR SEVERAL DAYS BETWEEN SUN AND FOGBANKS TO FIND THE GREAT SEAL HERD AGAIN...

JUST WHEN WE WERE GOING TO TAKE IN THE BOATS, SMOKE APPEARED ON THE HORIZON...

MAYBE IT'S A RUSSIAN CRUISER. ARE WE IN FORBIDDEN SEAS, CAPTAIN?

I DON'T WANT TO RETURN TO THEIR SALT MINES!

IT COULD BE WORSE, IT COULD BE MY BROTHER.

IT *IS* MY BROTHER!

INDEED, THE MACEDONIA, ARRIVING ON THE AFT STARBOARD, WAS RAPIDLY GAINING ON US....

THERE WAS NO SORT OF SALUTATION BETWEEN THE TWO BROTHERS WHEN THE STEAMSHIP OVERTOOK US. ON THE CONTRARY, WOLF GROUND HIS TEETH...

THE MACEDONIA CUT ITS BOILER BETWEEN OUR BOATS AND THE SEALS, AND LOWERED HER FOURTEEN BOATS IN THE SEA. THEY SWEPT UP THE HERD, ALMOST ENTIRELY RUINING OUR HUNT.

BAM BAM BAM BAM

THE BASTARD! HE'S GOING TO FILCH FIFTEEN HUNDRED DOLLARS FROM US! BROTHER OR NOT, I SHOULD KILL HIM FOR THAT!

DON'T BE SO MATERIALISTIC... WHO STEALS MY PURSE STEALS TRASH.

SHAKESPEARE, OTHELLO, ACT THREE, I KNOW.

LISTEN, I'M WILLING TO BELIEVE THAT IN THE MICROCOSM OF YOUR RELATIONSHIPS, EVERYONE BEHAVES WITH THOUGHTFULNESS AND CIVILITY. BUT HAVE YOU OBSERVED HOW YOUR CHARMING CIVILIZATION GIVES THE STRONGEST AND THE RICH THE ADVANTAGE AND OFFERS GLORY TO HE WHO CRUSHES THE OTHER?

I'VE SEEN FAMINE IN THE PORT OF LONDON AND THE DEATH OF SOCIAL REJECTS. YOU'VE HEARD OF THE TREATMENT METED OUT TO GENERAL KELLY'S UNEMPLOYED! YOU KNOW THAT, AT PRESENT, EUROPE IS TAKING UP ARMS, THE HIGH AND MIGHTY ARE PREPARING FOR A CONFLICT THAT LITTLE FOLK WILL PAY FOR WITH THEIR BLOOD.

SO, WHY DON'T YOU TOLERATE IN ME WHAT YOU ACCEPT FROM YOUR CIVILIZED WORLD?

XIII
7

THE FOLLOWING MORNING, EARLY, WOLF LARSEN APPEARED JOYFUL AND FIDGETY, ESPECIALLY WHEN THE WATCH ANNOUNCED THE RETURN OF THE MACEDONIA'S SMOKE...

HE HAD A PLAN. HE HAD THE CREW ASSEMBLE IN ORDER TO REVEAL IT TO THEM...

EVIDENTLY, HE WAS SPEAKING OF VENGEANCE AND HE REAPED CHEERING THAT SOUNDED LIKE ACTION STATIONS...

EVERYTHING WENT AS PLANNED. TAKING ADVANTAGE OF THE GREAT DISTANCE BETWEEN DEATH LARSEN AND HIS HUNTING BOAT, THE GHOST BORE DOWN AND DROPPED ALL HER BOATS IN THE WATER...

IT WAS A MATTER OF GRAPPLING ALL THE MACEDONIA'S BOATS AND MAKING THEIR CREWS CLIMB ON BOARD THE GHOST...

LIKE IT OR NOT, MOST OF THEM SURRENDERED RATHER QUICKLY...

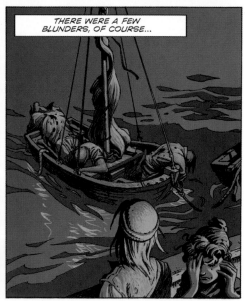

THERE WERE A FEW BLUNDERS, OF COURSE...

XIII
8

THAT WAS PREDICTABLE, MISS BREWSTER, BUT THE MOST PROBLEMATIC IS YET TO COME.

BOOM

BOOM

MY BROTHER HAS UNDERSTOOD WHAT'S HAPPENING! GET DOWN!

HELM FULL TO THE WIND!

MISS, IF YOU WOULDN'T MIND, DO GO BELOW!

I MAY CERTAINLY BE ONLY A WOMAN, BUT I CAN BE AS BRAVE AS YOU!

I LIKE YOU A HUNDRED PERCENT BETTER FOR THAT. YOU ARE FIT TO BE THE WIFE OF A PIRATE CHIEF.

XIII
9

THERE WAS NEED FOR HASTE. THE MACEDONIA, BELCHING THE BLACKEST OF SMOKE FROM HER FUNNEL, HAD ALTERED HER COURSE SO AS TO ANTICIPATE OURS...

THE HOPE FOR THE GHOST LAY IN THAT SHE SHOULD PASS THAT POINT BEFORE THE MACEDONIA AND TAKE REFUGE IN THE THICK FOG-BANK...

WHICH WAS BRILLIANTLY DONE BY WOLF LARSEN, A FINAL SHOT RICOCHETING NOT FAR FROM OUR STERN...

INSTANTLY, THE GRAY FOG FLOWED ON US LIKE A CURTAIN OF TEARS, AND THE HORIZON WAS LIMITED TO A FEW STEPS...

IN ABSOLUTE SILENCES, WE CARRIED OUT THE SKILLFUL MANEUVERS ORDERED BY OUR CAPTAIN AND DIDN'T SEE THE MACEDONIA AGAIN.

I'LL SERVE OUT PLENTY OF WHISKY TO THE HUNTERS AND PRISONERS. I'LL WAGER EVERY MAN JACK OF THEM IS OVER THE SIDE TOMORROW, HUNTING FOR WOLF LARSEN AS CONTENTEDLY AS EVER THEY HUNTED FOR DEATH LARSEN.

ARE YOU CERTAIN THEY WON'T TRY TO ESCAPE?

I HAVE MY OWN IDEA ABOUT IT.

AND NOW YOU'D BETTER GET FOR'ARD TO YOUR HOSPITAL DUTIES. THERE MUST BE A FULL WARD WAITING FOR YOU. AFTERWARDS, YOU GET TO BED, I'LL SEE TO EVERYTHING.

XIII
10

STRETCHED OUT ON MY BUNK, DESPITE THE CLAMORING OF THE DRUNKEN SAILORS, MY MIND WANDERED. I THOUGHT THAT IF EVER WOLF LARSEN, WITH HIS FEROCIOUS INSTINCTS, HAD ATTAINED THE SUMMIT OF THE LIVING, HE HAD ATTAINED IT THEN...

BUT MUCH HIGHER ON THE SCALE OF EVOLUTION I PLACED MAUD, MADE OF WIT AND REFINEMENT. HER EYES, HER MOUTH, HER VOICE!-- I, HENRY VAN WEYDEN, LITERARY CRITIC AND SCHOONER PILOT, WAS MADLY IN LOVE, I HAD TO ADMIT.

I KNOW NOT WHAT HAD AROUSED ME, BUT I FOUND MYSELF ON MY FEET, MY SOUL VIBRATING TO THE WARNING OF DANGER...

IN MAUD'S CABIN, THE MONSTER WAS THERE, FORCING HIMSELF ON HER!

AND I SAW RED AS NEVER BEFORE!

I TOOK A LITTLE WHILE TO UNDERSTAND. MY KNIFE HAD SLID ON HIS SHOULDER BLADE AND HAD, NO DOUBT, MADE NO MORE THAN A FLESH WOUND. A MIGRAINE HAD STRICKEN WOLF LARSEN...

LORD! LORD!

AAAAAARRRRH!

XIII
18

DRESS WARMLY, BRING AS MANY COVERS AS POSSIBLE, AND MEET ME ON THE DECK.

THE LAUGHING AND SINGING HAD QUIETED. I HEARD ONLY THE CREAKING OF THE SHIP AND THE LAPPING THAT CRADLED US...

LOADING SUPPLIES, CLOTHING, A RIFLE, CARTRIDGES, AND BARRELS OF WATER WAS RATHER FAST...

LOWERING THE BOAT WAS EASIER THAN EXPECTED...

SETTING THE SAILS, ON THE OTHER HAND, WHICH TOOK THE BOAT-STEERERS POSSIBLY TWO MINUTES TOOK ME TWENTY.

WE TURNED OUR HEADS TO SEE THE LAST OF THE GHOST. HER CANVAS LOOMED DARKLY IN THE NIGHT LIKE A FADING NIGHTMARE. THEN SIGHT AND SOUND OF HER FADED AWAY AND WE WERE ALONE ON THE DARK SEA.

XIII
13

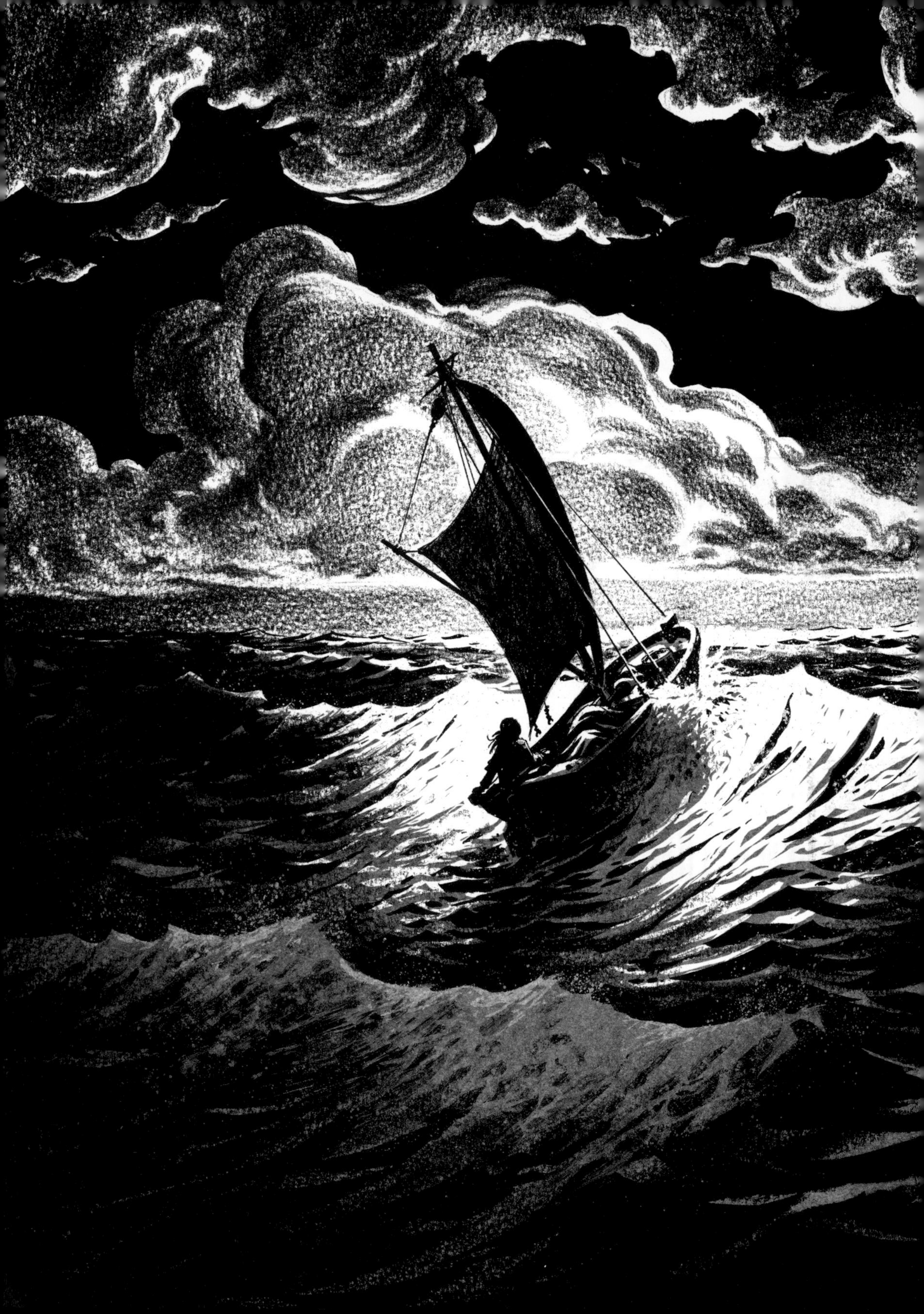

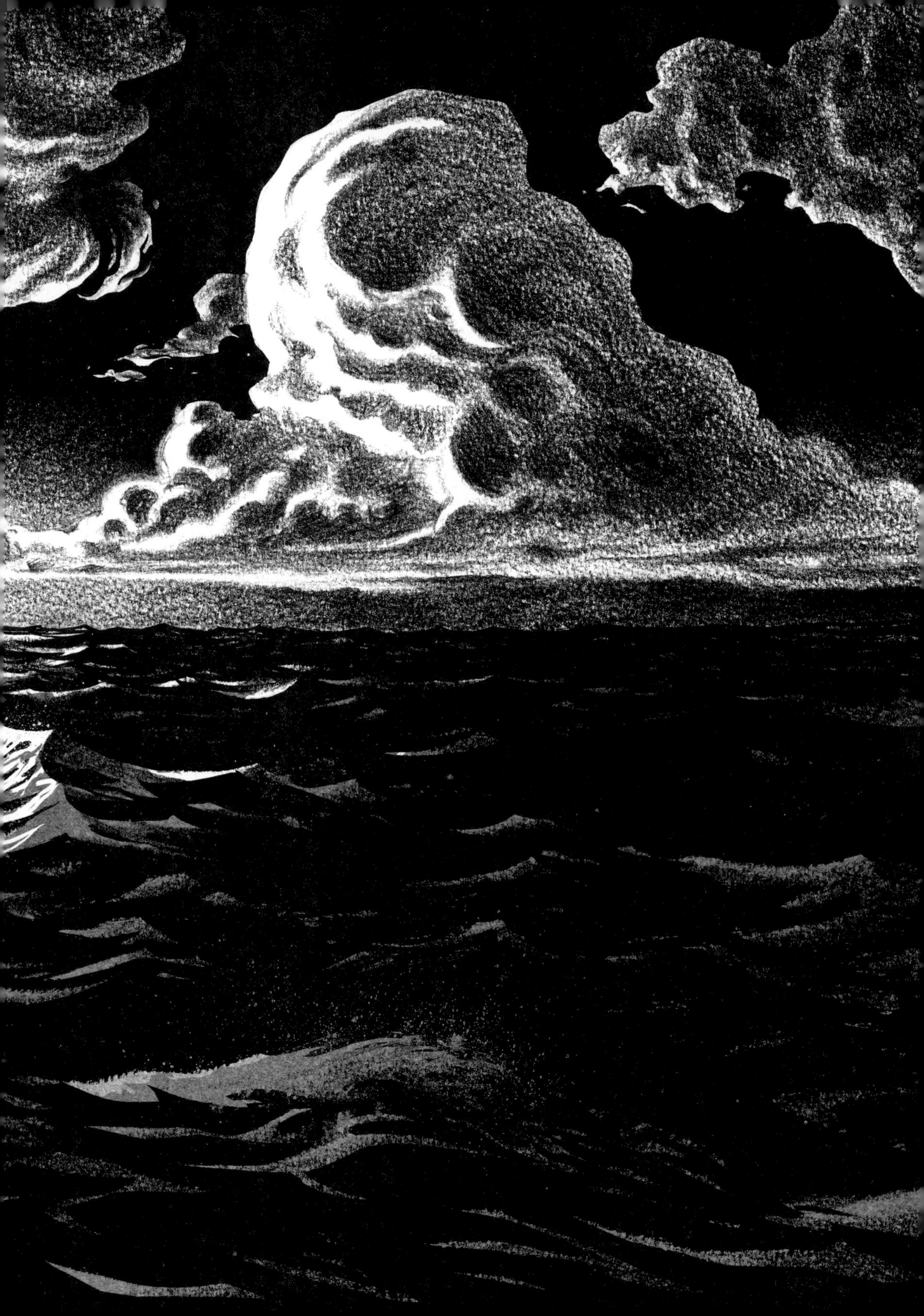

XIV

DAY BROKE, GRAY AND CHILL. THE COMPASS INDICATED WE WERE MAKING THE COURSE WHICH WOULD BRING US TO JAPAN...

GOOD MORNING, MR. VAN WEYDEN. HAVE YOU SIGHTED LAND YET?

NO, BUT WE ARE APPROACHING IT AT A RATE OF SIX MILES AN HOUR. IF THIS WIND SHOULD HOLD, WE'LL MAKE IT IN FIVE DAYS.

AND IF IT STORMS?

WE MAY BE PICKED UP ANY MOMENT BY A SEALING SCHOONER. THEY ARE PLENTIFULLY DISTRIBUTED OVER THIS PART OF THE OCEAN.

BUT PUT ON THIS OILSKIN. I'M GOING TO TEACH YOU TO STEER, ONCE WE'VE BREAKFASTED ON SOME DELICIOUS, COLD CANNED... TONGUE.

WHEN I LAID MY HAND AS DELICATELY AS POSSIBLE ON MAUD'S FOR HER FIRST NAVIGATION LESSONS, A QUIVERING WAVE IMMEDIATELY INUNDATED MY BEING TO THE BOTTOM OF MY HEART...

THE WARMTH OF HER GAZE, THE SWEETNESS OF HER GESTURES, THE SOFTNESS OF HER SKIN SEEMED SO UNREAL TO ME THAT I BECAME CONFUSED AND STUPID. SO MUCH SO, THAT THE WORDS OF A CHEAP ROMANCE NOVEL WELLED UP IN ME: "A FLOWER AMIDST THE THORNS..."

IN SHORT, SOMETHING NEW HAD AFFECTED ME: I HAD A REASON TO LIVE.

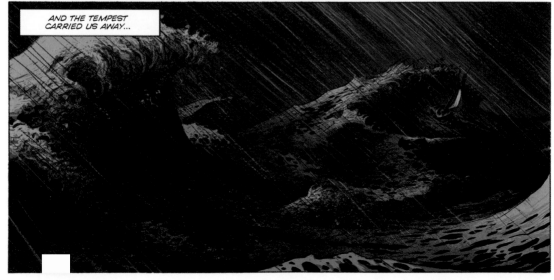

AND THE TEMPEST CARRIED US AWAY...

XIV
2

THERE IS NO NEED OF GOING INTO AN EXTENDED RECITAL OF ALL OUR SUFFERINGS DURING THE MANY DAYS THAT WE WERE DRIVEN AND DRIFTED, HERE AND THERE, WILLY-NILLY, ACROSS THE OCEAN...

I TRIED TO NOT REVEAL THAT OUR SITUATION WAS WORSE THAN EVER. WE WERE FARTHER FROM JAPAN THAN THE NIGHT WE LEFT THE GHOST. MY ESTIMATIONS... IN TRUTH, I WAS LOST, WE WERE DOOMED.

BUFFETED BY THE RAIN, DAZED BY THE WAVES, WINDBLOWN, I GAZED AT THE HORIZON BUT RARELY AND WEARILY. THAT'S WHY THAT JUTTING PROMONTORY, BLACK AND HIGH AND NAKED, AT FIRST SEEMED LIKE A HALLUCINATION TO ME...

WE STILL NEEDED LONG HOURS TO FIND A WELCOMING HARBOR...

I'D HAVE LIKED TO PRESS MAUD TO MY BOSOM AND CRY OUT ALL OF MY LOVE TO HER, BUT IF WE CLUTCHED ONE ANOTHER THUS, IT'S BECAUSE WE COULDN'T STAND ON OUR OWN. WE WERE BOTH SUFFERING FROM LAND-SICKNESS...

XIV
3

XV

IN THE MORNING, FOR LACK OF MATCHES, I MADE A FIRE WITH THE HELP OF A SHOTGUN SHELL. A CAN OF JELLIED PORK SERVED AS OUR COFFEEPOT...

MIRACULOUS! YOU'LL HAVE TO SELL YOUR RECIPE TO THE "GRAND CAFÉ" ON TAYLOR STREET.

HUM! 'FRISCO!--WHAT IF WE BEGAN BY VISITING THE ISLAND WHICH, POSSIBLY, DOESN'T APPEAR ON ANY MAP.

LET'S HOPE THIS PLACE IS LISTED AS A SEAL ROOKERY, IN WHICH CASE WE'LL FIND A STATION.

XV
1

A FISHING BOAT GAVE US A MOMENT OF HOPE...

BUT WE HAD TO FACE THE FACTS, THIS ROCK WAS ONLY INHABITED BY AMPHIBIANS AND SEAGULLS.

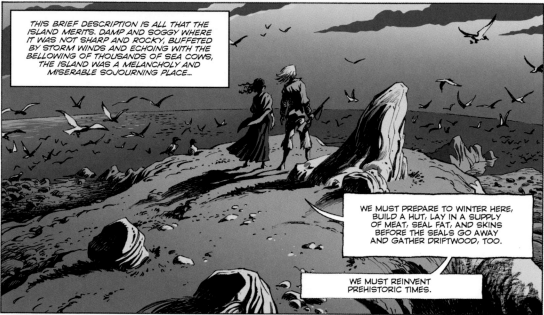

THIS BRIEF DESCRIPTION IS ALL THAT THE ISLAND MERITS. DAMP AND SOGGY WHERE IT WAS NOT SHARP AND ROCKY, BUFFETED BY STORM WINDS AND ECHOING WITH THE BELLOWING OF THOUSANDS OF SEA COWS, THE ISLAND WAS A MELANCHOLY AND MISERABLE SOJOURNING PLACE...

WE MUST PREPARE TO WINTER HERE, BUILD A HUT, LAY IN A SUPPLY OF MEAT, SEAL FAT, AND SKINS BEFORE THE SEALS GO AWAY AND GATHER DRIFTWOOD, TOO.

WE MUST REINVENT PREHISTORIC TIMES.

I'M READY TO COVER MYSELF IN FURS TO NOT DISPLEASE YOU.

PERFECT, FROM NOW ON, I'LL LET MY EYEBROWS GROW OUT!

XV
2

122

LIFE SOMETIMES BRINGS IMPROBABLE
CONTRADICTIONS. I WAS THE HAPPIEST OF MEN
DURING THAT HARD MONTH OF LABOR, BUT IN
ONE OF THE MOST DISAGREEABLE SITUATIONS...

IT WAS WITH A CERTAIN JOY THAT I WENT
TO KILL INNOCENT SEALS AND WITH
GREAT SHAME THAT I SAW MY "POETESS"
CUTTING OUT MEAT AND GREASE
AMID THE STEAMING, SMELLY GUTS.

I'D BUILT A CRUDE HUT AS A LOVE NEST
AND WE LOVED ONE ANOTHER IN THE
NAUSEATING ODORS GIVEN OFF BY
THE SKINS MAKING UP OUR ROOF.

IN FACT, EXCEPTING FOR MAUD,
EVERYTHING WAS HORRIBLE, BUT
I WAS PROUD OF LABORING TO
SHELTER HER FROM HUNGER
AND COLD FOR THE WINTER.

HOW COULD I HAVE CONFRONTED DAYS
SUCH AS THIS, IF I HAD NOT SPENT TIME
ON THE GHOST? HOW LONG WOULD THE
LITERARY CRITIC HAVE SURVIVED IF
HE'D BEEN SUDDENLY THRUST INTO
SUCH A HOSTILE ENVIRONMENT?

I WAS ON THE VERGE OF
THANKING WOLF LARSEN WHEN
THE SKY BEGAN RUMBLING
AS IF IN REPROACH...

XV
3

XVI

I WAS GLAD FOR HAVING SPENT THE NIGHT IN SAFETY, THINKING ABOUT THE POOR WRETCHES ON THE SEA. IT WAS A CLEAR DAY AND THE WAVES LAPPING ON THE BEACH ATTESTED TO THE FURY OF THE NOCTURNAL TEMPEST...

?

THE BLACK SCHOONER DIDN'T TAKE ME LONG TO IDENTIFY. WHAT FREAK OF FORTUNE HAD BROUGHT IT HERE? A DEATH-KNELL SOUNDED IN ME.

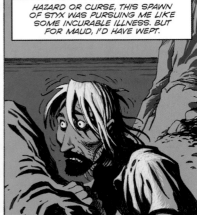

HAZARD OR CURSE, THIS SPAWN OF STYX WAS PURSUING ME LIKE SOME INCURABLE ILLNESS. BUT FOR MAUD, I'D HAVE WEPT.

XVI

MAUD! AWAKEN HER AND FLEE AGAIN! BUT FLEE WHERE? THIS ISLAND WAS TOO LITTLE FOR US TO HIDE THERE. COULD WE TAKE TO THE BOAT AND LOSE OURSELVES AGAIN ON THE WIDE RAW OCEAN?

AND WHY DID NOTHING SEEM TO BE STIRRING ON BOARD? HAD IT BEEN EVACUATED?

AT THIS STAGE, A DESPERATE DEED WAS AS GOOD AS ANY OTHER. I KNEW THIS SHIP. I HAD A SHOTGUN, MY KNIFE, AND IF I STUMBLED ON WOLF LARSEN, I WAS DETERMINED TO KILL HIM SUMMARILY, EVEN IF HE WERE SOUND ASLEEP!

NOT A SOUND, NO BREATHING, NO BODIES.

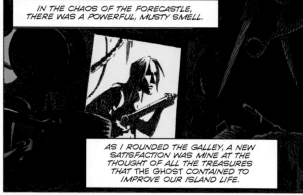

IN THE CHAOS OF THE FORECASTLE, THERE WAS A POWERFUL, MUSTY SMELL.

AS I ROUNDED THE GALLEY, A NEW SATISFACTION WAS MINE AT THE THOUGHT OF ALL THE TREASURES THAT THE GHOST CONTAINED TO IMPROVE OUR ISLAND LIFE.

?

CLAC CLAC

THE MONSTER WAS THERE, STARING AT ME, BUT SOMETHING WAS WRONG...

WELL? WHY DON'T YOU SHOOT?

COME NO CLOSER!

WHAT PLACE IS THIS? WHAT ARE YOU DOING HERE? WHERE'S MAUD?-- I BEG YOUR PARDON, MISS BREWSTER, --OR SHOULD I SAY, "MRS. VAN WEYDEN"?

DURING THE SUBSEQUENT CONVERSATION, I LEARNED THAT DEATH LARSEN HAD GOTTEN THE UPPER HAND BY BUYING OFF THE GHOST'S HUNTERS AND BY SUPPORTING A MUTINY. WOLF HAD BEEN ABANDONED TO THE HAZARDS OF THE CURRENTS IN THE SHIP, WITH ITS RIGGING DESTROYED.

A BLINDING HEADACHE PREVENTED THAT CURSED MAN FROM INFORMING ME ANY FURTHER...

XVI
3

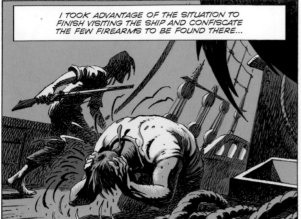

I TOOK ADVANTAGE OF THE SITUATION TO FINISH VISITING THE SHIP AND CONFISCATE THE FEW FIREARMS TO BE FOUND THERE...

BEFORE REJOINING MAUD, I APPROACHED THE CAPTAIN, WHO HAD LOST CONSCIOUSNESS, AND OBSERVED HIM.

HE WAS HAGGARD, HOLLOW-CHEEKED. THE EXPRESSION OF HIS EYES AND THEIR VERY ASPECT WERE SINGULAR...

ON OUR BEACH! HUMPHREY, WE'RE DOOMED!

ON THE CONTRARY, MAUD, WE'RE SAVED!

WE'RE GOING TO REPAIR *THE GHOST* AND SET OUT FOR JAPAN AGAIN.

AND WOLF LARSEN?

HE'S BLIND, I TELL YOU! AN ILLNESS IS DESTROYING HIM.

ARE YOU SURE OF THAT?

THE NEXT DAY, A VAST CONSTRUCTION BEGAN, WHICH WAS SPREAD OUT OVER SEVERAL WEEKS. I ALWAYS KEPT A WEAPON WITHIN REACH...

WOLF LARSEN WOULD APPEAR FROM TIME TO TIME, GENERALLY TO BASK IN THE OBLIQUE RAYS OF THIS SUN OF AUTUMN'S END...

TELL ME, WOLF, HOW DID YOU RECOGNIZE ME THE OTHER DAY, SINCE YOU'VE LOST YOUR SIGHT?

HA! HA! HA! BECAUSE THE ONLY IMBECILE IN ALL THE BERING SEA WHO'S UNABLE TO KILL A MAN WHO FRIGHTENS HIM IS NAMED HUMPHREY VAN WEYDEN!

I'VE TAUGHT YOU NOTHING! IF I'D BEEN A TIGER, YOU'D HAVE FIRED. HOWEVER, THERE'S NO DIFFERENCE BETWEEN THE LIFE OF A TIGER, THAT OF A MAN, OR THAT OF A FLY. DON'T YOU UNDERSTAND?

DARWIN CLEARLY DEMONSTRATED IT. IF EVOLUTION IS A TREE, MAN IS AT THE END OF ONLY ONE BRANCH AMONGST HUNDREDS OF OTHERS!

MAN WASN'T CREATED. HE'S AT THE SUMMIT OF NOTHING! THE HUMANITY YOU INSIST UPON IS NOTHING BUT POMPOUSNESS!

WE TRUSTED WOLF LARSEN SO LITTLE THAT WE SLEPT ON SHORE, TAKING TURNS STANDING GUARD, FEARING AT ANY MOMENT THAT HE MIGHT FIND THE STRENGTH TO LEAVE THE SHIP...

THE WORK WAS ADVANCING WELL. IT WAS CLEAR THAT, WITHOUT A TOPGALLANT, WITHOUT A MAINTOP, OUR SAILS WERE RIDICULOUSLY INADEQUATE FOR A SHIP SUCH AS THE GHOST. AN AMPUTATED BIRD THAT, WE HOPED, MIGHT LEAVE THE NEST.

XVI
5

IT WAS MAUD'S CRIES THAT AWOKE ME THAT NIGHT...

THE DEVIL NEVER ADMITS DEFEAT. HOW COULD I HAVE BEEN SURPRISED?

THE HUMIDITY OF THE NIGHT HELPED US PUT OUT THE FIRE.

XVI
6

THE PYROMANIAC WAS
LYING IN HIS CABIN...

I'LL KILL
YOU, HUMP!
KILL YOU!

MAUD! MAUD!

KILL YOU OR
RIP EVERY REASON FOR
LIVING FROM YOU!

-:AARR!:-

XVI
7

131

LUCKILY, THE FIRE HADN'T CAUSED ANY MAJOR DAMAGE. WE WERE DISCOURAGED, BUT WE HADN'T LOST HOPE. THAT'S WHAT WAS BREATHING ON THE EMBERS OF OUR LOVE.

I BOUND THE BEAST BY THE WRISTS. MAUD CAME REGULARLY TO FEED HIM IN THE BUNK WHERE I'D PLACED HIM.

WE HAD TO CHANGE SOME DRILLS, REDO THE MIZZEN SAIL, CURSING WOLF WITH EVERY GESTURE...

FINALLY, ONE NIGHT, PROFITING FROM THE COMBINED EFFECT OF A WIND FROM LAND AND THE HIGH TIDE, I SUCCEEDED IN TOWING THE BOAT AWAY FROM THE BEACH, READY TO SAIL AWAY...

WOLF LARSEN'S MOMENTS OF CONSCIOUSNESS WERE MORE AND MORE RARE. HE WAS HALF-PARALYZED. MAUD THOUGHT HE WAS SUFFERING FROM A BRAIN TUMOR...

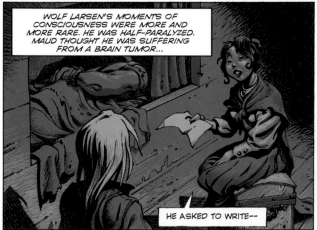

HE ASKED TO WRITE--

THIS MUST BE FOR YOU...

Immortality
BOSH

XVI
8

XVII

WE HAD TO SLIP THE ANCHOR IN THE DEPTHS
TO HAVE TIME TO BEGIN THE MANEUVERS OF
GETTING UNDERWAY AND AVOIDING BEING
PUSHED ONTO THE SHORE. THE GHOST
SEEMED TO START IN TO LIFE...

MY NEW LITTLE CABIN BOY PUT
ALL HER HEART INTO IT AND
HOISTED THE JIB AS THOUGH
THE MOON WERE AT THE END.
THE SAIL FILLED. THE SCHOONER
HESITATED THEN VEERED AWAY
ON THE OTHER TACK. VICTORY!

PERHAPS MAUD COULD HAVE DESCRIBED THE POWER
AND MULTITUDE OF FEELINGS THAT OVERWHELMED
US AT THAT INSTANT: JOINED TO ONE ANOTHER, THE
GRIM COVE OF THE SEAL ISLAND BEHIND US, OUR
FUTURE ON THE HORIZON BRIEFLY REPAINTED IN
THE COLORS OF OUR HOPES BY A BRAVE SUN..

SO, HUMPHREY, IS
THAT THE END OF
PREHISTORY?!

YES, THE BEAUTIFUL
LIFE OF GALLEY SLAVES
FOR US NOW!

THE MAKESHIFT SAILS WERE UTTERLY
CLUMSY, BUT THE SHIP WAS FOAMING
ALONG AND RIDING THE WIND...
A LITTLE TOO WELL, NO DOUBT...

XVII
1

THE WIND WAS FAVORABLE AND THE OPEN SEA BECKONED TO US. I TRIMMED EVERYTHING FOR THE QUARTERING BREEZE TOWARDS JAPAN AND RESOLVED TO RUN AS LONG AS I DARED...

UNFORTUNATELY, WHEN RUNNING FREE, IT IS IMPOSSIBLE TO LASH THE WHEEL, SO I FACED AN ALL-NIGHT WATCH.

MAUD, UNABLE TO STEER IN A HEAVY SEA, COMFORTED ME REGULARLY AND LOOKED AFTER WOLF, TOO.

THROUGHOUT THE DAY, THE WIND INCREASED. IT WAS TOO GOOD TO LOSE, BUT BY NIGHTFALL I WAS EXHAUSTED. A THIRTY-SIX HOUR TRICK AT THE WHEEL WAS THE LIMIT OF MY ENDURANCE AND THE SEA UNLEASHED ITSELF ONCE AGAIN...

IT WAS RELUCTANTLY THEREFORE THAT I HEAVED TO. BUT I HAD NOT RECKONED UPON THE COLOSSAL TASK THE REEFING OF THE SAILS MEANT FOR ONE MAN.

THE WIND BALKED MY EVERY EFFORT, RIPPING THE CANVAS OUT OF MY HANDS AND IN AN INSTANT UNDOING WHAT I HAD GAINED BY TEN MINUTES OF SEVEREST STRUGGLE. TWO HOURS FOR THE FORESAIL AND THREE HOURS MORE WERE REQUIRED TO GASKET THE MAINSAIL AND JIB!

AT THE TIPS OF MY HANDS HARDENED INTO HOOKS, MY FINGERS LOOKED LIKE BRUSHES DRIPPING WITH BLOOD. LIFE NEAR BUFFETED OUT OF ME, I PLUNGED INTO THE DARKNESS...

XVII
2

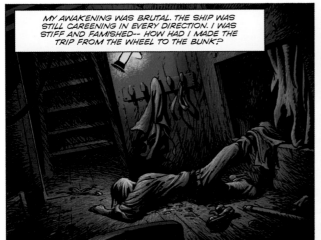

MY AWAKENING WAS BRUTAL. THE SHIP WAS STILL CAREENING IN EVERY DIRECTION. I WAS STIFF AND FAMISHED-- HOW HAD I MADE THE TRIP FROM THE WHEEL TO THE BUNK?

HOW LONG HAD I SLEPT? IT WAS A SLEEP-WALKER MAUD GUIDED AND SUPPORTED.

MAUD...

MAUD!

MAUD!

MAUD?! MAUD?!

WOLF LARSEN!

XVII
3

135

KILL ME OR TEAR EVERY REASON FOR LIVING FROM ME! THAT'S IT, EH?!

WHAT HAVE YOU DONE?

I DISCOVERED HER IN THE STEERAGE, BY WOLF LARSEN'S BUNK. HIS LIFE HAD FLICKERED OUT IN THE STORM.

WOLF LARSEN HAD BEEN HURLED DOWN FROM THE TOPMOST PITCH OF LIFE TO BE BURIED ALIVE AND BE WORSE THAN DEAD.

FREED OF THOSE SHACKLES, HIS SOUL WAS FREE NOW. BUT IN TRUTH, HE HAD ALWAYS BEEN FREE, AS MUCH AS ONE CAN WHEN ONE IS IGNORANT OF THE FEELING OF GUILT.

XVII
4

WHEN I HAD HOISTED WOLF LARSEN'S BODY ON DECK READY FOR BURIAL, THE WIND WAS STILL BLOWING HEAVILY...

MAUD WAS SURPRISED AND SHOCKED, BUT THE SPIRIT OF SOMETHING I HAD SEEN BEFORE IMPELLED ME TO GIVE SERVICE TO WOLF LARSEN.

XVII
5

I REMEMBER ONLY ONE PART OF THE SERVICE AND THAT IS, "AND THE BODY SHALL BE CAST INTO THE SEA."

XVII
6

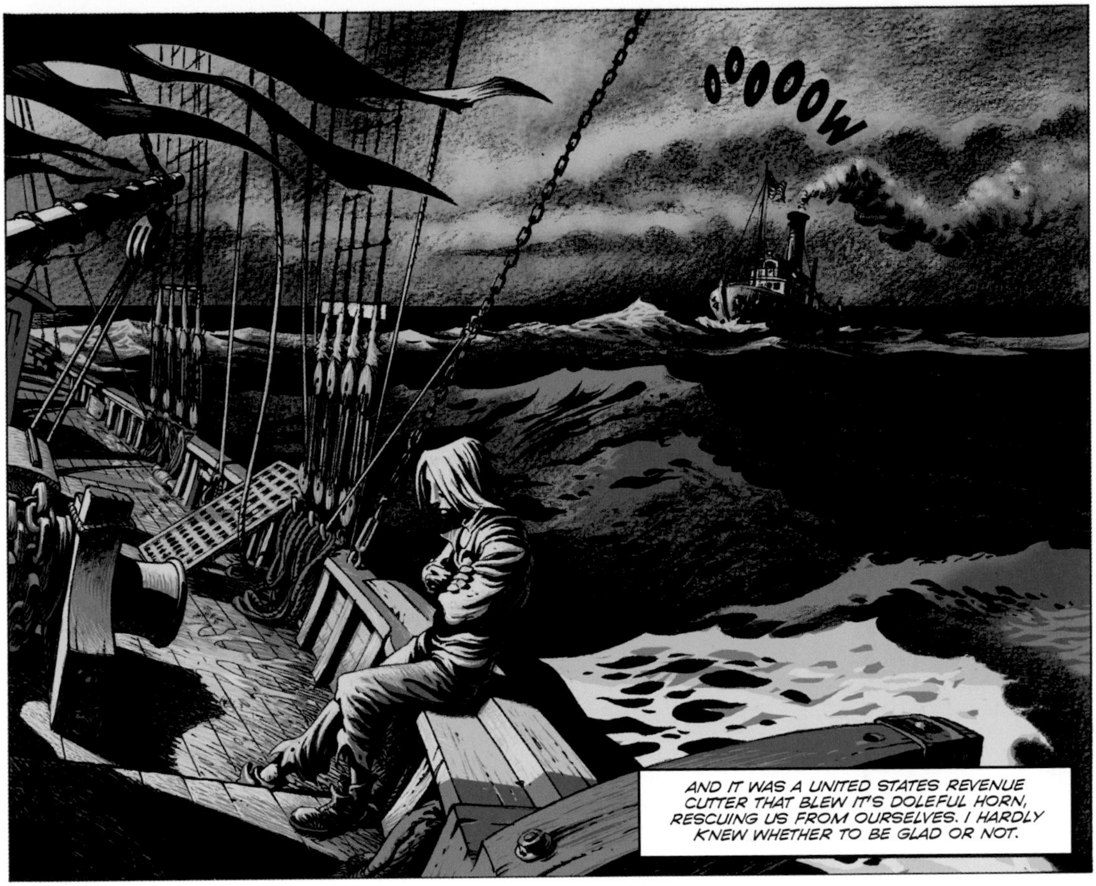
OOOOOW
AND IT WAS A UNITED STATES REVENUE CUTTER THAT BLEW IT'S DOLEFUL HORN, RESCUING US FROM OURSELVES. I HARDLY KNEW WHETHER TO BE GLAD OR NOT.

END

WATCH OUT FOR PAPERCUT**Z**

Welcome to the exciting, engrossing eleventh CLASSICS ILLUSTRATED graphic novel from Papercutz, the company dedicated to publishing great graphic novels for all ages. It's funny—there are times when I'm convinced words have lost their meaning, and the term "all-ages," may be a case in point. You see, many times when I tell folks that Papercutz is publishing material for "all ages," they automatically assume that means "children." While children are certainly a part of our target audience, we don't want to exclude adults either. Just as a movie studio such as Pixar is able to produce animated films that appeal to both children and adults, we strive to reach that same audience.

Further compounding the problem is that bookstores like to be able to shelf books by the age of the intended audience of each and every book, and "all-ages" is way too broad a category for them. Does it go in the children's books section or the adult books section? If that wasn't enough, they're constantly dividing those sections into more sections. For example, there's Young Adult, and there's even a new section called "New Adult." I suppose there may be a section for me soon called "Old Adult." As much as I love bookstores, this continues to confound me.

Speaking of which, I suppose I should introduce myself. I'm Jim Salicrup, the Editor-in-Chief of Papercutz. These days I spend way too much time worrying about whether books such as this beautiful adaptation of Jack London's The Sea-Wolf by Riff Reb's will wind up shipwrecked on the Children's Section's shelves or will it wash ashore on the shelves of the generically labeled "Graphic Novel" Section, to truly be rescued by literature-lovers off all ages?

This particular graphic novel really does potentially appeal to all ages—with an exciting adventure story balanced out with truly thought-provoking moral conflicts. Traditionally, CLASSICS ILLUSTRATED would run a black caption after the last panel of every adaptation advising: "Now that you have read the CLASSICS ILLUSTRATED edition, don't miss the added enjoyment of reading the original, obtainable at your school or Public Library." (These days, we should add: "Or online.") While Riff Reb's adaptation is rather faithful to Jack London's original novel, there are pages and pages of dramatic debating between Wolf Larsen and Humphrey van Weyden that would've been difficult to translate to comics—unless you simply had page after page of the two of them talking (not unlike some of the sequences in the our previous volume's Poe adaptations)—that have been significantly reduced or even eliminated. Just as film will focus on the visual aspects of the source material when adapting novels, so do graphic novels—as both film and comics are visual media. So, in cases such as The Sea-Wolf there really is "added enjoyment" to be found in the original. Which is not to say, this adaptation can't "stand on its own legs."

There's truly nothing more heart-breaking to an editor than publishing a great book, and failing to find an audience for it. Riff Reb's adaptation of Jack London's The Sea-Wolf is a great book, and I sincerely thank you for finding it! We greatly appreciate your support, and hope you stick with us when CLASSICS ILLUSTRATED DELUXE #12 presents Jean David Morvan and Jian Yi's adaptation of "The Monkey God."

Thanks,

Jim

Stay in Touch!
EMAIL: salicrup@papercutz.com
WEB: www.papercutz.com
TWITTER: @papercutzgn
FACEBOOK: PAPERCUTZGRAPHICNOVELS
FAN MAIL: Papercutz, 160 Broadway, Suite 700,
           East Wing, New York, NY 10038

CLASSICS ILLUSTRATED GRAPHIC NOVELS
AVAILABLE FROM PAPERCUTZ

#1 "GREAT EXPECTATIONS"

#2 "THE INVISIBLE MAN"

#3 "THROUGH THE LOOKING-GLASS"

#4 "THE RAVEN AND OTHER POEMS"

#5 "HAMLET"

#6 "THE SCARLET LETTER"

#7 "DR. JEKYLL & MR. HYDE"

#8 "THE COUNT OF MONTE CRISTO"

#9 "THE JUNGLE"

#10 "CYRANO DE BERGERAC"

#11 "THE DEVIL'S DICTIONARY AND OTHER WORKS"

#12 "THE ISLAND OF DOCTOR MOREAU"

#13 "IVANHOE"

#14 "WUTHERING HEIGHTS"

#15 "THE CALL OF THE WILD"

#16 "KIDNAPPED"

#17 "THE SECRET AGENT"

#18 "AESOP'S FABLES"

CLASSICS ILLUSTRATED graphic novels are available only in hardcover for $9.95 each, except #8-18, $9.99 each. Available from booksellers everywhere.

Or order from us. Please add $4.00 for postage and handling for the first book, add $1.00 for each additional book. MC, Visa, Amex accepted or make check payable to NBM Publishing.
Send to: Papercutz, 160 Broadway, Suite 700, East Wing, New York, NY 10038.

papercutz.com

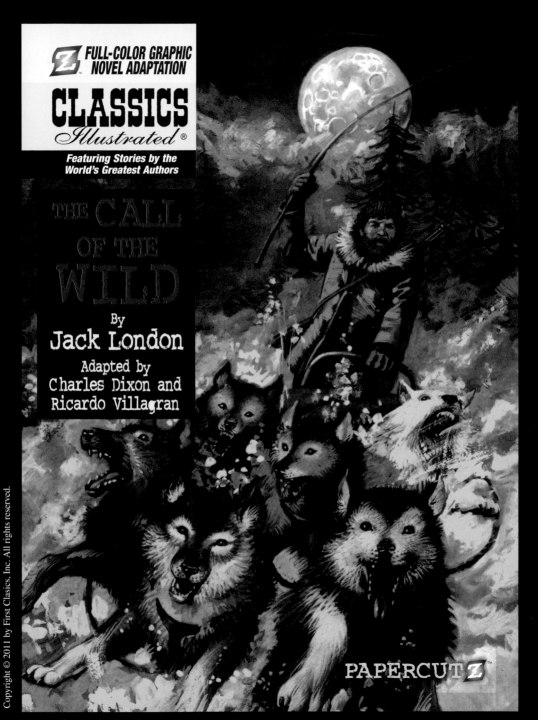

JACK LONDON
(1876-1916)

Jack London was born in San Francisco on January 12, 1876. He was raised in poverty along the Oakland waterfront; to help support his family, London sold newspapers and performed odd jobs. At the age of 14, London quit school and went to work full time in a cannery. His love of boys' adventure fiction influenced him to turn pirate at the age of 16, when he used his sloop *Razzle Dazzle* to raid oyster beds in San Francisco Bay. In an example of the contradictions which were later to inform his fiction, the next year found him working alongside the harbor police to stop such piracy. After spending a year at sea on a sea-hunting expedition and traveling the country as a tramp, London finished high school and briefly attended the University of California. In 1897, he joined the Klondike gold rush. Although success in the gold fields eluded him, the experience gave him valuable insight into the rugged individualists who populated the raw frontier. London returned to Oakland and took up writing; he sold his first short story, "To the Man on the Trail," to the Overland Monthly in 1898. By 1900, he had published enough of his tales of the Yukon to warrant a collection, *The Son of the Wolf*. London's stories of the vigorous and often brutal life in the far north found a ready audience, and his style – raw, excitable, but always readable – was successful among both young and old. His fame was assured when *The Call of the Wild* was published to great acclamation in 1903. A passionate believer in socialism and a champion of the working class – views advocated in such novels as *The Iron Heel* (1908) and *The Valley of the Moon* (1913) – London nevertheless also subscribed to Nietzche's cult of "red blood." Much of London's fiction, including *The Sea-Wolf* (1904) and *The Abysmal Brute* (1913) is populated by characters stripped of social conventions to reveal the unhuman that lies beneath the veneer of civilization. The Darwinian concept of survival of the fittest is also a recurrent theme in his fiction. London published 51 books – all well received – during his 17-year writing career, but his later works never achieved the popularity of *The Call of the Wild*. Frustrated by what he perceived as his failure, and plagued by bouts of alcoholism and rheumatism, London died in 1916 at the age of 40. In a eulogy, his daughter, Joan, described London – along with Stephen Crane and Frank Norris – as "the three young pioneers who at the turn of the century had blazed the literary trail into modern American literature.